About tomorrow...

ABBI GLINES

Copyright © 2020 by Abbi Glines

All rights reserved. This book or any portion thereof may not be reproduced or used in any manner whatsoever without the express written permission of the publisher except for the use of brief quotations in a book review.

Printed in the United States of America
First Printing, 2020

Abbi Glines Publishing
P.O. Box 3130
Peterborough, NH 03458
www.abbiglinesbooks.com

Editing by Fairest Reviews Editing Services
https://fairestofallbookreviews.blog/fairest-reviews-content-editing-copy-editing-proofreading-services/
Cover designed by Damonza
https://damonza.com
Interior Design by The Illustrated Author Design Services
www.theillustratedauthor.com

To everyone who needs hope for tomorrow…

acknowledgments

This was the first book in YEARS that I wrote in less than a month. That used to be my "thing" I could write 'em fast. Being able to do that again was amazing. I had time to get lost in my characters and for that I must thank my family first.

Britt went above and beyond with taking up the slack so I could lock myself away. He not only did his work but most of mine too. He is a super hero. He will also hate that I said all this. Hopefully he doesn't read it.

Ava and Emerson had to hear "Mom is working. I can't right now." For the most part they didn't complain. Emerson had her moments. Ava was a trooper though...although she's been on this ride since 2011 and knows the score.

My older children who live in other states were great about me not being able to answer their calls most of the time and they had to wait until I could get back to them. They still love me and understand this part of mom's world.

Danielle Lagasse for being there, for being a writing buddy and friend in my new life here in New England. She's made moving easy. Her family has become part of ours.

My editor **Becky Barney at Fairest Reviews Proofreading Services**. She once again made my story shine. I'm thankful I found her.

My formatter who also did my book trailer- **Melissa Stevens at The Illustrated Author**. Her works is always amazing.

The Next Step PR who deals with all the shit I toss their way and manages to make me appear organized. Kiki Chatfield was the first person to read this book and I love her for it! They are a great team to work with and I'm thankful they helped me pull off yet another release.

Damonza for my book cover. It is perfect and I love it.

Abbi's Army ALWAYS. Y'all are what keeps me sane when I release a new book. Thanks for always supporting me.

My readers- without you there would be no one to read my stories. I get to write because y'all read. I love you all!

MAY 25, 2010
PORTSMOUTH, NEW HAMPSHIRE

"Did you ask him?" Cora whispered beside me.

"No, but why me? Why can't you?" I asked. Creed was her brother and it was her idea to walk to town for ice cream. I felt weird asking him. He was busy.

Cora rolled her eyes at me. "Because he won't say no to you," she replied.

Frowning I glanced back at her brother, Creed Sullivan, and Jack Tate who had moved five houses down the street from the Sullivans this past fall. Jack was Creed's new best friend. Last summer and all the summers before, Creed had always spent his days with me and Cora. This year things were different. Sure, he did some things with us, but he was with Jack more and more. They were currently playing basketball on the Sullivans' driveway. I didn't want to just go up and interrupt them. Things with Creed felt different now and our friendship wasn't the same.

"When they're done playing maybe they'll want to go," I suggested to Cora.

Cora sighed dramatically. "If *you* ask, Creed will want to go now. If my mother wasn't being ridiculous, we would just go by ourselves, but she thinks Creed going keeps us safe. Like, seriously, what is he gonna do to protect us?"

Creed was dribbling the ball when he noticed us watching them. He paused and studied me a moment. I hated feeling like this with Creed. Why had things had to change? It had been so much easier before. This year things were too different. When I looked at Creed, my stomach did funny things and my cheeks felt warm. I liked him and not just as a friend. I *really* liked Creed Sullivan. In the past, I had always thought he was cute, but this year when he had smiled at me the first day I'd arrived at my Gran's, I felt a little faint.

"Hey, Creed!" Cora called out to him, realizing he was looking this way.

He shifted his gaze to his sister. "Yeah?"

"Sailor wants to go get an ice cream in town, but mom says you have to go with us." Cora told him, which was not true. I wanted to crawl in the bushes and hide from embarrassment.

Creed looked back to me and I knew my face was bright red. I could feel it. "You want ice cream?" he asked me.

I was about to tell him it could wait until he was done or that I didn't actually need an ice cream when Cora jabbed me so hard with her elbow, I was sure it was going to leave a bruise. Wincing, I managed to nod my head.

"We're in the middle of a game," Jack said, stating the obvious.

Creed shot him a look I couldn't see, then he turned back to me. "Okay, let's go," he said.

"You're kidding? Jeez, dude, I know she's hot but bros over…"

"Don't finish that sentence," Creed warned him.

"Told you," Cora said under her breath in a sing-song voice. "My brother likes you, likes you."

"No he doesn't. Stop that," I whispered, hoping to God he didn't hear her.

"Even Jack's noticed," she added then winked at me.

Jack had said I was hot. Did Creed think I was too? The butterflies in my stomach started up again and I felt so awkward. I missed the days when being around Creed didn't make me a ball of nerves.

Creed threw the ball at Jack, who caught it and made a umph noise.

"Can I come?" Jack asked.

"No," Creed said, but he was looking at me. "Ready?" he then asked me.

I nodded then remembered I needed to go get money from Gran. "Can I go by Gran's and get money first? Y'all can keep playing."

"Y'all," Jack repeated, laughing at me. He made fun of my accent a lot.

"Shut up," Creed said, glaring at his friend.

Jack rolled his eyes. "Whatever. Call me when you're done with her."

Creed walked toward Cora and me. "I have money. You don't need any," he told me.

"Oh really, you can pay for mine too," Cora told him in a sweet voice.

"You have your own money," he said.

Cora nudged me again and said, "tell him to buy my ice cream too."

I wished she would stop saying things like this around Creed. He may be her twin brother, but he wasn't mine. I didn't want to make him irritated with me. "I can go to Gran's and get money for both of us," I told her, while begging her with my eyes to stop embarrassing me.

"That's okay. I'll pay for hers too," Creed said.

Last year I would have laughed about this and we would have all but run to town for ice cream. How did one year change us so much?

"Wicked cool! Let's go get ice cream." Cora beamed brightly, having gotten her way, and headed down the sidewalk without waiting for us to follow.

A corner of Creed's mouth lifted in a crooked grin. "She's a brat. You know that. Come on," he said.

I relaxed a little then. This was Creed. We had built forts together, baited fishing hooks together, had sleep overs in backyard tents. He wasn't a stranger. He was just beautiful now. Maybe he always had been. I was just realizing it this year. That was the difference.

We fell into step following Cora. This summer I had spent more time alone with her than I ever had. We weren't a trio anymore. Creed had Jack and I missed him. Moments like this, when he did something with us, made the world feel right again. The Sullivan twins were the best part of my year, and I only got to be with them in the summers.

Creed's hand touched mine and my breathing hitched. Had that been an accident? We were walking close and maybe his hand had accidentally brushed mine. Before I could think too hard about it, his hand slipped over mine and his fingers threaded with my own.

We were holding hands. My heart was going haywire and the smile stretching across my face was impossible to control. I wanted to look at him but I was afraid to. Creed Sullivan was holding my hand.

He squeezed it then and I turned my head and had to tilt it back a little to look at him. Another difference this year was he was now four inches taller than me. He had gotten beautiful and tall. He met my gaze and grinned at me.

"What? Don't look so surprised," he said.

I raised my eyebrows but said nothing. He was holding my hand. Of course, I was surprised.

He shifted his eyes to his sister, who thankfully hadn't looked back to see us holding hands. "She may be a brat, but she's right. I'd do whatever you asked me to do."

one

OCTOBER 24, 2019
BOSTON, MASSACHUSETTS

I'd always heard that nothing compared to New England in the fall. This was my first experience at seeing it first-hand. My life in New England had been in the summers- when the private school I attended was closed and my mother ran off to Europe. Summers were the best part of my year. I didn't harbor any bitterness that my mother had no time for me in the summer. She'd given me my summers with Gran.

"It's stunning, isn't it?" Griff asked.

I simply nodded. I wasn't sure words could describe it. Leaves of every color it seemed covered the cobbled streets. Looking from the beauty around us, I inhaled the brisk fall air. Griff chuckled and I glanced up at him. He was equally stunning. From the first moment I'd met him, I'd been struck by how handsome he was. He was almost six-feet-tall and had a lean build from running. Griff ran in marathons, but I couldn't run down the driveway without having to stop and catch my breath. His dark hair was always styled perfectly. My hair was unruly with curls I struggled to contain, and I envied his smooth dark locks. Hazel eyes that could only be described as dreamy looked down at me. Griff Stafford hadn't been my first love, but he'd been my savior, even if he didn't realize it. I adored him.

"Come on, I can't wait until you see this place." Griff grabbed my hand and led me to the front door of the apartment building. Griff had left Nashville two months ago to get settled in before his classes started. I'd had packing and other things to set into place. Now that we had both graduated from Vanderbilt University, our lives were different, busier. Having time for us was a luxury we didn't get anymore.

Griff had four years of medical school ahead of him. I had my Gran's house. My bachelor's degree in Art History would hopefully help me find a job at an art museum. Moving to my Gran's house in Portsmouth, New Hampshire, had never been something I considered until recently. I had done some research on art museums close to Portsmouth and I was even willing to drive to Boston for a job, if I could find one. Working in Boston meant Griff and I could have lunch together. It would be perfect and worth the commute.

While I'd been in Nashville packing up my life and trying to stay clear of my mother, Griff had been in Boston. He was happy here and I knew moving to Gran's house was the best decision for our relationship. I didn't see how we'd see each other much if I'd stayed in Nashville. Not that I wanted to stay there. It was just the memories connected to my time at Gran's were complicated and I didn't know if going back, six years later, would feel like it was just yesterday or if it had been enough time to heal.

The building had been here a long time, but it was well-kept. There were only ten apartments, and the structure had been refurbished from a boarding house built in 1875. Griff flashed me a grin over his shoulder. "Luckily we're on the third floor and not the fifth."

At each landing, there were three doors. Griff had told me on the phone that there was only one bathroom on each floor. I wasn't sure I'd like that very much. The pro was that the majority of the other residents in the building were students at Ashurst Medical Center, like Griff and his roommate. They were unlikely to have any loud parties in the building to disturb their studies. I still wouldn't want to share a bathroom with them though.

Griff opened the door to his apartment and motioned for me to go inside. I loved it instantly. The apartment had the charm of early last century. Even with furnishings chosen by Griff and his roommate, the place had a warm character to it. Much like my Gran's house did in Portsmouth. The difference here was the "city posh" feel to the location.

"This is the main living area. My room is this way," Griff said grinning. He knew I loved it here without asking what I thought. I followed him across the room to the first door on the left. "Chet's room is over there. His cousin is coming today to stay for a week or so off and on. They're going to share the room, which should work out fine since he has a bigger room. Mine is the smaller one, but my rent is a hundred less a month than his."

His door opened and the simplicity of it was perfect. There was a full-size bed in the far-right corner up against the wall. His large overstuffed and faded blue chair sat in the other corner. It had been his grandfather's chair and he was attached to it. The chair had been the only furniture he moved here. The rest he'd bought when he arrived. This was my first time seeing it; although I'd asked him to send pictures, he never got around to it.

One single floor lamp stood beside his chair. A black three-drawer dresser sat against the left wall with a black framed mirror hung above it. Beside that were book shelves full of his textbooks and other medical journals. All he needed was an area rug and I made a note to buy him one. The floors would be cold soon.

"This is amazing," I said, tilting my head to look up at him. He smiled then bent his head to kiss me. He was happy here and I was relieved. I felt as if he'd chosen Boston because of the proximity to my Gran's house. I hadn't been sure what to do with her house, but the idea of selling it had been too painful for me to consider. When he had chosen Boston for med school, I'd made my decision easily enough.

Now, I got to live in it and start my life in New England. Far enough away from my mother and her insanity to find some peace. No one knew me here; I wasn't known as the famous country singer, Denver Copeland's, daughter like I was in Nashville. I could just be me.

The door to the apartment opened and a male voice began talking. I hadn't met Chet yet and knew little about him. Griff had been so busy since moving here, our talking had been limited.

"Room's to the right. Your bed is the one on the left," I heard him say. He wasn't alone.

"You get to meet both my roommates," Griff said, looking pleased.

Then *he* spoke…The other one…the new temporary roommate. Time slowed and I stood there unable to move. Breathing seemed difficult. My heart was the only thing moving quickly… too quickly. Butterflies erupted in my stomach and although I knew it wasn't true. It wasn't him. The voice…it was so similar. Deeper now but the tone, the accent, it was the same. I was going to hyperventilate if I didn't focus on getting myself under control. It was just a voice. Nothing more. Emotions churned in my chest, overwhelming me, and I still couldn't move.

Griff's hand found mine and I heard him say, "Come on," as if my world hadn't just been tossed into a churning sea of memories, both good and bad. I took a deep breath and closed my eyes briefly. It had been six summers since I'd seen him. Six years since our lives changed without notice. Why did Creed Sullivan still affect me so much? It wasn't fair that the sound of a voice could do this to me.

I needed to see the stranger's face and I knew my emotions would stop going crazy. I just needed reassurance that it wasn't Creed. Once all I'd wanted was to see Creed Sullivan again. I had wanted to ask him why, have him hold me, promise me he still loved me but that Sailor was no longer. The one thing I had overcome was loving Creed.

That reassurance I had hoped for never came because the stranger wasn't a stranger.

When my eyes found his face, it felt as if time stopped. All the memories were back and the last moment I had been held by him slapped me in the face. Years of counseling seemed pointless. I was going to fall apart. Jerking my gaze from him, needing to find composure and quickly before Griff noticed, I looked at the other man in the room. The one I didn't recognize. The face that wasn't in my dreams and nightmares. The face that didn't haunt me.

"Hey! I didn't know you were here and this must be Sailor," a guy with a headful of blonde curls and bright green eyes said as he stepped forward and held out his hand. "Nice to meet you, Sailor. I'm Chet. I've heard a lot about you, and Griff wasn't exaggerating. You're as lovely as he said you were."

Keeping my gaze on Chet and forcing a smile was difficult. The heat from the other set of eyes in the room felt as if they were burning a hole through my head. How did we do this? What did we say? I managed to form words that made sense. "Thank you, it's nice to meet you too. I feel as if I know you already." I lied. Griff didn't talk about Chet a lot. He hadn't talked about much at all. Most of our calls had been short.

Chet then nodded his head toward the other body in the room. Although, I didn't need an introduction. "This is Creed Sullivan, my cousin. Creed, this is my roommate, Griff Stafford, and his girlfriend, Sailor Copeland."

Griff stepped forward and held out his hand to Creed. "Nice to meet you," he said, and once again, my body reacted to the sound of his voice.

"Likewise," Creed said.

I placed another smile on my face that I didn't feel and shifted my focus from my boyfriend to the one boy I thought I'd love forever, Creed Elijah Sullivan. His gaze was already on me and he gave me a smile that seemed almost mocking. It wasn't genuine. He held out his hand to me and I stared at it a moment before slipping my hand in his.

He gave me a firm handshake. "Pleasure to meet you as well, Sailor." And that was it. He dropped my hand and stepped back. His dark hair was longer than I'd ever seen it and tucked behind his ears. He gave me a nod then walked off toward his new bedroom.

Chet chuckled and shook his head. "Creed is a moody musician. You'll get used to him," he said.

"No worries," Griff replied. "I've given Sailor the tour so we are headed to get some dinner. Want me to grab you anything? Or Creed?"

"No thanks, I've got a date with Chelsea, the girl from the coffee shop I told you about. Don't worry about Creed," he paused and shrugged, "he will go out when he's ready."

I looked back at the bedroom door Creed had closed behind him. He was taller, his jaw was more defined and there was stubble on it, his voice was deeper. Six years had changed both of us. I may look older now, but he knew me. He could pretend that he didn't and if that was what he needed to do then fine, but Creed knew me. Too much had happened between us for him to forget my name.

I'd already lived through him shutting me out completely as if it were my fault Cora was dead. I never understood why he'd turned on me and refused to speak to me. Both our worlds had changed the day we found Cora. It hadn't been our fault. No one had any idea the demons she had been battling. She'd not told us. Never mentioned it. Yet, Creed had refused to speak to me or acknowledge my existence as if Cora's overdose was my fault. I'd lived with that pain until one day I was different. I wasn't that girl anymore. He couldn't still hurt me. Time hadn't healed everything I realized. My heart wasn't fully recovered. The ache was there, stretching and waking up from it being lodged down as deep as I could suppress it.

two

OCTOBER 25, 2019

I was reluctant to leave the warmth of the bed. I'd woken briefly when Griff's alarm clock had gone off two hours ago. I didn't remember him leaving though. I'd slept right through that. We hadn't stayed up late because he had an early class today, but the travel yesterday had worn me out. The movers would arrive at my Gran's in two days. I was staying with Griff until my things arrived. Her house wasn't empty, since she'd left everything in it to me, but I wanted my things to be there too. I wasn't ready to walk into Gran's house with just her things there…and no Gran.

I smelled the wood burning in the fireplace, and if Griff had been the last one to poke it then I needed to go tend to it before the fire died. I wasn't an expert at lighting fires, so I got up and grabbed the fleece rob Griff had left out for me. Wrapping it around my shivering body, I hurried and pulled on some thick fuzzy socks before going into the living area of the apartment.

Thanks to the fire, the living room was at least fifteen degrees warmer than the bedroom had been. The flames coming from the fireplace also didn't look as if they'd been ignored for two hours. The large fresh logs burning meant I wasn't alone.

There were two options as to who had kept the fire going. Glancing around the room and over the top of the divider into the small kitchen space, I saw no one. The other bedroom door was closed. Maybe they were gone now. I had no idea if Creed was in college or had a job or what he did other than he was a musician. That much I expected. Creed had been playing the guitar and writing his own songs since he was ten years old. He'd gotten his first guitar for Christmas that year, and by May, when I arrived for the summer, he had mastered several songs and written one of his own.

Cora would sing with him. She had sung beautifully. I used to love listening to them. The sadness came with her memory as it always did. She was the closest thing I had to a sister. She was the only best friend I'd ever had. We told each other all our secrets or I thought we had until the day we found her. I didn't want to think about that. I'd spent years in therapy dealing with her death. Seeing Creed brought back darkness that I'd fought hard to overcome.

I didn't want to go back to that place in my head. It was about my focus. I would get some coffee then curl up in a chair beside the fire and make a to-do list for when I got to Gran's. Focusing on my immediate future and not letting my past come back to haunt me.

The kitchen was small but well-stocked as far as coffee supplies went. There wasn't much else in the way of nourishment. Unless you counted a bottle of ketchup, a block of cheese, and some stale bread as food. I was impressed with Chet and Griff's supply of creamer and sugar. Making coffee the way I liked it, with too much sugar and cream, made my morning infinitely better. I stopped off in the bedroom to grab a pen and my notebook, before finding a spot on the sofa close to the fire.

It wasn't even Halloween yet and it was freezing. This was crazy and something I'd need to get used to living here. In

Nashville, they weren't even wearing long sleeves yet. Unless a random cold front came in for a couple days, no one would need sleeves until November. It didn't make me miss Nashville though. The only bright spot in my life there had been Griff.

"Morning," a deep voice said and my head snapped up from the flames I'd been staring at. I'd known he was probably here, but I hadn't been prepared for this, for talking to him or being alone with him. Hearing his voice again sent my stupid body into a weird turmoil. As if it had missed the sound and wanted to hear more of it. Why did it want to hear more of it? It would only bring me pain. My brain and I were in agreement. It was the rest of me that was confused.

Creed had put on a pair of faded jeans and a vintage Def Leppard t-shirt, but he'd not brushed his hair. It worked for him, but then Creed was the kind of sexy that could wear anything and still turn heads. As a little girl, I'd loved playing with him, and as a teenage girl, I had fallen in love with him.

"Hello," I said so softly, it was almost a whisper.

"Their coffee is shit," he said, as he walked toward the kitchen.

I turned my gaze back to the fire. Pretending like we were strangers was difficult. Once there had been so much I wanted to say to him. I'd wanted to ask him why? What had I done wrong? Why had he turned on me without a reason?

Now, he was here. We were in the same room and I had no words. I couldn't think of one thing to say.

I heard him in the kitchen and as much as I wanted to not care that he was here, my body was attuned to his every move. Maybe it was my nerves or uncertainty. It couldn't possibly be more than that. His footsteps were soft and I realized he must be barefoot. The cold wouldn't affect him like it did me. He was a New Englander.

He sat down in the chair across from the sofa and his gaze was on me. I didn't want to look at him. The fire was less confusing and unsettling. I didn't have to pretend with the fire. Creed, however, was a different story. How did he expect me to act like we were strangers when there was so much in our past?

"You sure you're ready for a New Hampshire winter if you're already freezing?" he asked me.

I turned my head to meet his gaze then. "How do you know I'm moving to New Hampshire?" I asked him.

He smirked. "I asked." That was it. All he was saying was that he asked.

"Why?" I shot back. If we were "strangers" then why did he care?

He sat his cup of coffee on his knee and gave a small shrug of his shoulders. "Hell, Sailor, I don't know. Maybe because yesterday I was coming to stay with Chet and try out playing with this new band and the next thing I know you come walking back into my world. I was fucking curious," he replied.

I watched him as he took another drink of his coffee before responding.

"You acted like you didn't know me," I said, pointing out the obvious.

The corner of his lips curved ever so slightly. "Yeah, well, I don't know about you, but rehashing our history together in front of those two didn't sound like a good time to me."

Okay. That did make sense. If he'd let on that we knew each other, they would have wanted to know the details. Griff would have wanted more than I'd be willing to share. He would have wanted to know why I never told him about Creed and Cora. I wouldn't have been able to explain that without possibly hurting him. I turned my focus back to the fire and drank my coffee.

We sat in silence for several minutes. I didn't know what to say or if there was anything to say. Our past needed to stay in the past, and although I felt like I was lying to Griff, I couldn't talk about Creed and Cora. I'd never been able to talk about the Sullivans. Not to anyone other than my therapist and she had forced it out of me.

"Best if we keep the past to ourselves," he said breaking the silence.

I nodded my head and didn't look at him.

He stood up then and I wondered if I'd ever be alone in the same room with him again. This would be my only chance to ask him the questions that had not only hurt me but had broken me. I had this moment and I knew I wouldn't take it. It no longer mattered. I had moved on from Creed Sullivan. He wanted to forget and so did I.

"Griff seems like a nice guy," he said as he stood looking down at me.

I nodded. "He's a great guy," I told him and forced a smile. If no other truth could be told that one could. I'd been lucky when Griff walked into my life. He had been everything I needed. He had saved me when nothing else had worked. Loving Griff was easy.

I didn't watch as he walked away. The bedroom door closed and I knew I was alone in the room again. I had a list and some phone calls to make. Thinking of Creed Sullivan was in my past and I would not bring that back up.

I picked up my pen and opened my notebook, just as the first strum of the guitar came from the other room. Pausing, I let myself remember how his face looked when he played. It had once been one of my favorite things to see.

Creed stopped playing after an hour and fifteen minutes. I had given up trying to make a list and taken my overnight bag to the community bathroom. Luckily it was available and I had plenty of time to get a shower and put on some makeup. When I walked out of the bathroom there was a woman outside the apartment door texting something on her phone. She glanced up at me and did a once over then went back to her texting. I needed her to move so I could get inside the apartment but the tall, dark-haired, stunning female with eyes that reminded me of a cat was apparently busy.

When I stood there not moving and trying to politely wait for her to finish her text conversation, she glanced back up at me and, this time, she was scowling with annoyance. "Can I help you?" she asked with a snide tone that was uncalled for, considering I was the one who should be annoyed.

"Yes, if you could let me get inside that would be nice," I replied as politely as I could.

She looked at the door then back at me. "This is your apartment?" she asked.

"No. It's my boyfriend's," I replied, although this was not her business.

"Who is your boyfriend?" She snapped her eyes now looking ready to attack me. They were almost glowing. Calm down cat girl.

"Griff Stafford," I answered her although I should have told her off. I was too nice. It was one of my worst traits.

"Must be a roommate," she said. "I'm looking for Creed Sullivan. He gave me this address."

Ah. Okay. This girl did not seem like the kind of girl Creed would be involved with. He was nice. Or he had been nice. This female was scary. I didn't know Creed now though. He'd changed. Not only had his looks gotten more rugged but he was different.

"He's inside. Or he was when I went to get a shower," I told her.

She stepped back and waved at the door. "Well, can you open it? He didn't give me the code."

I didn't want to open it. It would seem Creed had bad taste in women. Not for me to decide although it was disappointing. I walked past her and pressed the four numbers I was sure she was memorizing. Then opened the door and walked inside. Creed was, once again, in the chair beside the fire. His left ankle was propped up on his right knee and a book lay open in his lap. He lifted his gaze and didn't look pleased or surprised.

"You didn't hear me knock?" the female demanded, pushing past me and into the room.

"Hello, Ember," he drawled and closed the book he had been reading.

She placed her hand on a very narrow hip. "Why tell me to come over if you're not going to answer the damn door?"

I walked past them and headed for Griff's bedroom. I needed to find somewhere to go. It was time I got on a coat and went for a walk.

"I didn't tell you to come over. I recall giving you the address when you asked me."

"That's the same thing. Why would I ask for your address if I wasn't coming to see you?"

I heard Creed sigh. "You're right. I'm glad you're here now."

I scrunched my nose up as I pulled on a coat and added a scarf. She did not sound pleasant to be around at all. Granted she was stunning but yikes. Sometimes beauty is not enough. This is one of those times. Then again, maybe she was sweet as sugar when no one was around. What did I know? Not your business Sailor.

Slipping my feet into a pair of boots, I grabbed my camera and headed for the door. I had wanted to take pictures of the colorful leaves and the pumpkins on the doorsteps yesterday. Now, I had plenty time to do it. I walked out of the bedroom to find Ember was sitting in Creed's lap and they were kissing. I swung my gaze off them and headed for the door.

"You leaving?" Creed asked.

I didn't look back. "Yep," I replied then opened the door to get the heck out of there.

three

"Shelly isn't going to pull it off. We all know it. I'm still stunned she got this far," Chet said, before putting a fork full of Caesar salad in his mouth.

"I've got two in Gross Anatomy that I can't figure out how they got in either," Griff replied.

I had been sitting silently and listening to them talk about other medical students for over fifteen minutes. Chet seemed to have a thing for this Shelly because although he was bashing her, he couldn't shut up about her. I didn't think she needed to be judged for dancing on a pole. She was paying for medical school. I commended her for smart planning.

"You want more Fettuccini?" Griff asked me then.

"No thanks," I replied then looked back longingly at the fire in the living room.

He chuckled. "Go get warm. I'm almost done and I'll join you and bring some wine."

Relieved to be released from listening to Chet's complaining about poor Shelly, I got up and headed for the warmth of the fire. Picking up a throw on my way there, I snuggled into the sofa and sighed. I'd spent more time out in the cold today than I'd wanted, but I hadn't wanted to come back here and interrupt anything. The colors of the leaves had been breathtaking and made the freezing temps worth it. I'd been distracted by them at least.

"Did Creed keep the fire going for you this morning?" Chet asked from the kitchen.

"Uh, yes, he did," I replied.

"He doesn't get cold easy. He grew up in New Hampshire and that breed can take some cold ass weather," Chet said.

Griff laughed. "You're from Rhode Island. Is it really that different?"

"Hell yes. I'm from the warmer New England climate."

I seriously doubted there was such a thing. They continued to talk as I watched the flames and enjoyed the warmth under the fluffy throw. I wasn't sure how much time had passed when Griff took the spot beside me and pulled me to his side. Chet sat down in the chair across from us and they continued with their talk about classes and professors. I listened some, but my eyes felt heavy and closing them was all I wanted to do. It was comfortable and safe with Griff. I'd missed him and being here with him again made everything seem like it was normal. Almost. There was the issue of Creed.

I was woken up when Griff picked me up from the sofa.

"You need help?" I heard Creed's deep voice but the room was dark.

"I'm awake. I can walk," I told Griff.

He pulled me tighter against his chest. "I got you now," he said. "Can you open the bedroom door?" he then asked Creed.

I felt silly being carried and wondered how long I'd been asleep. The fire was no longer lighting up the room with a glow. All I heard was the embers crackling as it slowly faded. "You don't have to carry me," I said again.

"I want to," Griff replied.

We walked into the bedroom and the door closed behind us. Griff placed me on the bed and then went to get my cotton leggings and flannel pajama top. "Are you going to dress me too?" I asked then yawned.

He grinned and handed me the clothing. "If I undress you, I won't be interested in putting clothing back on you and you're tired. Better let you dress yourself."

I almost told him I wasn't too tired for sex but I didn't. Something about Creed being in the other room made me feel strange. Creed had been my first and my only other sexual partner. I didn't want to think about why it made me feel wrong. I just wanted to forget Creed and go back to sleep.

OCTOBER 26, 2019
BOSTON MASSACHUSETTS

I hadn't expected to wake to an empty bed this morning. It was Saturday and Griff didn't have any classes. After stretching and giving myself adequate time to get fully awake, I made the sprint from the bed to the chair to get the robe and fuzzy socks. Today would be a good day to buy him that area rug for this room. The floors were already freezing.

The living room was quiet but it wasn't empty. Griff was sitting on the sofa with a large book in his lap, his glasses on, and a highlighter in his right hand. He was so engrossed in what he was doing, he didn't look up when I opened the bedroom door. Chet was sitting in the chair also reading from a large medical book with a notebook and a pen beside him. They were studying. Griff had said he was already sick of all the memorizing and reading he had to do. This was supposed to be the hardest year of medical school and for his sake I hoped it was.

I didn't speak for fear of interrupting something important. Instead I went to the kitchen to make coffee. While I was busy doing that, I heard another door open and I knew without looking who had joined us. Creed's presence here made this uncomfortable. As much as I had missed Griff, I was looking forward to moving into Gran's tomorrow. Staying here was difficult. Surely in time it would get easier.

"Must be fascinating shit they're reading," Creed's deep voice said as he entered the kitchen.

I forced a smile and took my cup of coffee to move out of his way. I went to the table and sat down, wishing I could get closer to the fire but afraid to disturb them. I didn't watch Creed but I was aware of his every move. That needed to stop. My body was reacting as if I was seventeen again.

Ignoring it and him wasn't going to change things. I had to rewire my brain where he was concerned. I turned to look at him then and he was standing in front of the refrigerator with it open. I already knew there wasn't much food in there. Griff and Chet ordered out often. There was a list of their favorites with menus and phone numbers in the first drawer to the left of the fridge.

"I don't think they buy food. Just coffee supplies," I whispered.

He glanced at me then back at them. "Appears so," he replied, not whispering as he closed the door. "Guess I'll go find food. Want to come?"

I hadn't been expecting that question. It was polite. If I was rewiring my brain to stop remembering who Creed once was to me and seeing him only as Griff's roommate then I should go. It seemed normal enough. No big deal that I'd had sex with Creed before or that I loved him once. Shouldn't matter that it took me until Griff to get over the pain of losing him.

I shook my head. "No, that's okay. I'd have to get dressed and I'm not awake enough for that or the freezing temps out there."

He shrugged. "Fine but you're going to need to toughen up. Portsmouth is fucking cold in the winter."

Words felt lodged in my throat. Me remembering was one thing. My quietly acknowledging our past was easier than hearing him speak of Portsmouth. The place where all our history together existed. The sooner I left this apartment and moved north the better.

Creed seemed oblivious to my inner turmoil. He walked over to the coat rack and grabbed his coat then slipped on some boots.

"Can I get anyone something to eat or does everyone just require ketchup and cheese to survive?" Creed asked.

Griff glanced up then from his book. His gaze went to me. "Hey, babe, you're awake."

I smiled at him. He could completely zone out when he was studying.

"Where are you going?" Chet asked. "The Bagel Hut two blocks over has wicked avocado stuffed bagels."

"Anyone else?" Creed asked.

"Sailor? You want something? There's a menu for The Bagel Hut in the drawer," Griff said. "I'd like BCT bagel," he then told Creed.

Creed looked back at me. "I want some decent coffee. Can you go with me and help me carry all this shit?" He didn't mind spending time with me. It was so easy for him. I didn't affect him at all and that was good…but it hurt. I hated that it hurt. I didn't need to affect him. He lived with my boyfriend who I loved. It was best that he was unaffected.

I couldn't say no. I stood up. "Give me a sec to change and grab my coat," I replied.

Creed nodded and I hurried to put on my jeans, sweater, coat, gloves and scarf. While doing so, I gave myself a pep talk. I could do this. No big deal. Getting used to being around Creed was required. Six years, Sailor. It's been six years. You're different now. Taking a deep breath, I glanced at my reflection in the mirror. I could do this.

Griff looked up from his book again when I walked out of the bedroom. "My cash is in the top drawer in there," he told me.

"I have my debit card in my pocket. I'll get it," I replied then walked over to him and bent down to kiss him. His hand touched my face gently.

"I promise this afternoon we will go do touristy things," he said as I stood back up.

"Okay," I said with a smile. Then made my way over to the door where Creed stood waiting. Watching me. His expression was one I couldn't decipher.

"Are you warm enough?" he asked me then and an amused smile touched his lips.

"Hopefully," I replied.

He opened the door then and motioned for me to go first. We walked in silence for a few minutes. It was starting to get awkward but maybe just for me.

"How long have you been with Griff?" he asked.

"We met second semester our freshman year at Vanderbilt," I told him.

"How did you meet?" he asked me then.

Smiling at the memory, I replied, "I walked into the wrong dorm room on my way to a study group. Griff was on the phone lying on his bed. I had been so embarrassed but he'd ended his call and we had ended up going out for coffee. I never made it to my study group."

"Sounds like you," he said simply.

I stopped smiling. His comment wasn't meant to upset me. I knew that. But it did. If he didn't want to remember and he wanted to keep things in the past then he needed to not reply as if he had that kind of knowledge. He didn't know me. Not really. Not anymore. That girl was no longer.

The Bagel Hut had a line out the door. "Figures," he muttered.

Most of the good places to eat had lines. I glanced around and saw no other option with a shorter line. Maybe it would move quickly.

"Will you freeze?" he asked me.

"Possibly," I replied.

He chuckled and one of the girls in front of us glanced over her shoulder, got a good look at Creed then nudged her friend, whispered in her ear and the other girl glanced back at him. Creed, however, wasn't paying attention. He had crossed his arms over his chest and was leaning back against the building watching the activity on the street with a bored expression.

I understood why they were looking at him. I looked away. Appreciating the view was off-limits for me. He wasn't a stranger on the street. The past made me feel guilty for looking.

"Is your mother still crazy?" he asked me then.

I nodded. Creed knew more about my mother than Griff. I'd wanted to start over when I went to college. When I'd met Griff, I kept most of my sordid family life from him. I wanted to forget it, so I never spoke of it.

"Sorry to hear about your Gran," he said. His mother had come to the funeral. I'd mentally prepared myself to face him again but he'd not come. The blow hadn't been as hard because Griff had been by my side. Part of me was relieved he hadn't come to the funeral.

"It was sudden. As hard as that was I'm thankful she didn't suffer," I told him. That had been how I had dealt with losing her. Reminding myself that although I hadn't gotten a chance to say goodbye at least she didn't suffer from a terrible disease that killed her slowly. "She was asleep. It was peaceful."

He studied me a moment and I felt self-conscious having his focus on me. The line moved and we moved up with it. One of the girls did another glance back at Creed then me before turning around. I was sure she was trying to figure us out. We didn't look like a couple. There was too much space between us for starters. If he were Griff, I'd be snuggled up to his side.

"When was the last time you were there?" he asked.

"To see Gran or in Portsmouth?"

"Both," he clarified.

"I saw Gran three months before she passed away. She came to Nashville for Christmas. The last time I was in Portsmouth was for the funeral."

"I was there last month. My mom decided to move back. She and her husband, Chet's uncle, bought a house on Dearborn," he told me even though I hadn't asked. The line moved again.

His parents had divorced and moved from their home beside Gran about six months after Cora's death. Although I hadn't come back to Portsmouth that next summer, I knew they'd moved that winter. Gran had told me. Before Cora's death, our plan for that summer had been for the three of us to hike the Appalachian trail. Not the entire thing but start in Maine and go as far as we could before we all went to college that fall. I'd forgotten that until now.

"Where did y'all move after…" I couldn't finish the question. I glanced up at him, wishing I hadn't asked that or mentioned it.

"My dad moved to Simsbury, Connecticut. Mom moved to Burlington, Vermont, to live near her mother," he replied but said nothing more. There were so many things I could ask him but I didn't. I didn't need to know about his life. He was no longer a part of mine. We would rarely see each other after I left tomorrow. I didn't need to know which parent he lived with after the divorce.

When the line moved again, we were finally inside the warmth of the Bagel Hut. I sighed from the pleasure of it. A small grin lifted the corners of Creed's mouth. The girls in front of us both turned around this time. The blonde was smiling at Creed, but the other girl's focus was on me. They must have listened to us enough to know we weren't a couple and were ready to make their move on Creed.

"Excuse me but I need to know," the brunette asked, looking directly at me. "Are you Sailor Copeland?" she asked. The other girl was looking at me now too.

This wasn't new. I was used to this, in Nashville. It had never happened in New England. I'd loved that about coming here in the summers. I opened my mouth to respond, but Creed spoke first.

"Who?" he asked.

The brunette looked more unsure now than she had before. She studied me again then glanced at him. "Sailor Copeland. Denver Copeland's daughter," she said, and I saw a couple people turn to look at us. Crap.

"Whose Denver Copeland?" Creed asked.

The girl looked at him like he was crazy. "The country singer, CMA entertainer of the year, several times over," she said the words like he should know this.

He laughed loudly then and nudged my arm. "Does your pops sing, Nyx?" he asked me.

I wasn't used to denying who I was. Not because I wanted attention but because I was a terrible liar. However, a few of the other people who had turned to look at us had turned away now. Creed was a much better liar than me.

I shook my head but didn't say anything for fear I'd mess up this ruse.

"Last I checked her pops sat at a desk all day balancing books," he told the girl then flashed a smile that I was sure could melt any female in a hundred-mile radius. She turned her attention to him then and gave him a seductive smile.

"I'm Sierra," she told him.

"Dan," he replied with a nod. The line moved then and it was their turn. "Better order up," he told her then winked.

He had her so flustered she forgot her order and her friend kept giggling. I shot him a grateful smile and waited for them to get their order in so we could finally make ours. Before they moved out of the way the blonde turned around and handed "Dan" a napkin. "Call me," she said then licked her lips before walking over to the pickup window. The extra sway to her hips as she walked was slightly over the top.

Creed ordered for everyone but me and I added my request for an avocado with over easy egg bagel. He pulled out a card to pay and I handed him my debit card. He shook his head. "I got this."

Frowning, I put my card away but didn't like him paying for everyone's meal. "I'll pay you back for ours at the apartment. I don't have cash on me right now."

He didn't respond and when we moved over to the pickup window, the girls had already gotten their food and had to move out of the cramped area. Creed took his cup and went to get some of their coffee. I doubted theirs was any better than the coffee at the apartment. I didn't say anything though. Standing in line at a coffee house was the last thing I wanted to do.

On our walk back to the apartment, Creed was quiet. He didn't mention the girls or his covering up my identity. The silence no longer felt awkward. It was comfortable. I welcomed it. We had talked enough. When we arrived at the house their apartment was in, he opened the door for me to go inside.

"Thanks," I said.

"Here, take these," he replied, handing me the bag.

I took the bag and he reached inside to take out his bagel. Once he had his, he said "Later." Then let the door close before he walked away. That was odd.

I took the food up to the hungry med students and tried to think about anything other than my conversation with Creed.

four

The movers had called right before lunch to tell me that the moving van had mechanical issues. They were going to unload it and move everything to another moving van. This was going to put them two days behind schedule. Once Griff knew he had more time with me in Boston, he spent three more hours on his studying.

Instead of staying in the apartment, I went and bought groceries, made lunch for both Griff and Chet then went shopping for a rug. After finding the perfect area rug for Griff's bedroom, I went back to the apartment to find Griff was in the bathroom. Chet had said he was getting a shower and we were all going to Red's tonight to hear Creed play.

Creed was trying out with a band tonight that played at several of the local college bars. He hadn't come back to the apartment all day, at least while I was there. Going to see him play wasn't what I wanted to do. However, it was rude to tell Griff I didn't want to go. I thought about faking a headache.

"Thanks for the food," Chet called out from the kitchen.

"You're welcome. Thanks for letting me stay a couple extra days," I replied.

"Hell, if you want to stay and buy the groceries and cook I am good with that," he said.

Griff walked back into the apartment then with damp hair and a freshly shaven face. I sighed in appreciation. He was so nice to look at and he was mine. He gave me a wicked grin. "Keep looking at me like that and we won't get real far," he teased.

Chet laughed and walked out of the kitchen with a sandwich and a bag of chips in his hands. "At least let me get to my bedroom first."

Griff saw the food in his hands. "She has us set up I see," he said then smiled back at me.

"Hold on tight to her pretty boy because I'm in love," Chet replied.

"You're going to need to get over it. She's taken," Griff said.

Chet made an exaggerated pout. "How will I go on?"

A knock at the door interrupted his teasing. Griff turned around and opened it. A scantily dressed blonde beamed at him. "Hiya, I'm looking for Creed. Tell him Jazz is here," she said.

Jazz? Was she serious? Who had a name like Jazz?

"Uh, he's not here," Griff replied then looked back at Chet.

Chet walked over to the door and Griff moved away then turned and came toward me.

"He expecting you?" Chet asked then finished chewing the large bite of sandwich in his mouth.

"Yes. We are going to the gig together," she said then added, "I'm the lead singer in Kranx."

"Ah, okay, well come in and he should be here soon I guess. You might want to text him. Haven't heard from him in a while," Chet told her.

"Thanks but I can't. I've got to get going. I'll call him," she said then spun around on her red heels and walked away.

Chet closed the door and then turned back toward us. "Jazz seems high maintenance," he said and rolled his eyes.

Griff chuckled and kissed my head. "I'm going to go get changed."

I probably needed to change too.

"You might want to eat something before we go tonight. Red's isn't known for their menu. It has colon cancer stamped all over it," Chet told me then took a bite of the banana in his hand.

"Colon cancer?" I asked confused.

He shrugged. "You know fried greasy shit."

"Oh!" I replied.

He grinned. "I sound like a doc already," he replied looking smug.

The door to the apartment opened then and Creed came walking inside. Fighting not to look his way was difficult. He was hard to ignore.

"Jazz came by, you weren't here, she left," Chet told him then sank down onto the sofa.

Creed nodded but his attention was on the banana Chet was eating. "Where did you get a banana?" he asked.

Chet pointed it in my direction. "Beautiful here went grocery shopping. We have legit food in the kitchen."

My eyes met Creed's as he shifted his attention to me. "You're leaving tomorrow," he stated. I assumed he was pointing that out because I'd bought food.

"We get to keep her a few more days. Movers are having mechanical issues," Chet answered for me. I was thankful for that. Talking to Creed after being apart from him for any given time was hard. I didn't want it to be hard. I wanted to look at Creed the same way I looked at Chet.

Creed said nothing but headed toward his bedroom. When the sound of the door closing behind him clicked softly, I was studying my hands. I didn't watch him walk. Things always felt awkward. For me. Not him.

"He's a moody dude," Chet said from the sofa across from me. "Always has been or as long as I've known him he has been."

That got my attention and I lifted my gaze to meet his. "He's your cousin," I stated the obvious.

Chet nodded. "Yeah, but he hasn't always been. His mom married my dad's brother four years ago."

Oh…okay. Thinking of his mother married to someone else was odd. The last good memory I had of his parents, his mother was baking banana bread and his father was teasing her about her cooking skills. They'd seemed happy. I'd never witnessed them fighting, and I spent as much time at their house as I did my Gran's over the many summers I visited.

Chet leaned forward, resting his elbows on his knees. "His parents got divorced when he was seventeen just a few months after his sister died. Sad shit," he whispered. "I figure it's part of his moodiness. I just overlook it."

I watched as Chet stood up then turned to look back at the closed door of his room. He and his dad had been so close. My chest ached for him. I knew so little about his life after Cora died.

The door to Griff's room opened and I remembered that things happened for a reason. If Creed hadn't shut me out then I wouldn't have found Griff. I loved Griff. He was good to me. He made me happy. I'd been so unhappy when we met.

Because of losing Creed and Cora.

Shaking my head, I cleared my thoughts. I wasn't going to think about what could have been. There was no point. Life happened and time moved on.

five

Red's was loud and college students were everywhere. It reminded me a lot of Smokey's in Nashville. All college bars probably looked alike. This was just my second one to visit. However, Red's was on the water, making the view much nicer.

Griff's hand stayed closed around mine as we walked through the people. Chet was leading the way and he had said there was a table reserved for us near the left of the stage. I found that hard to believe with the mass quantity of bodies in this bar.

When we finally broke through the congestion of people there was, in fact, a table to the left of the stage. It was a round booth to be exact. The table was large enough for at least ten people to sit around it with eight of those people fitting in the curved booth seating.

I recognized Jazz sitting snuggled up to a guy with spiked bleach-blonde hair on the right side of the booth. A guy with black hair pulled back in a ponytail sat on the far-left side of the booth and on a stool beside him with one booted foot propped on the stool and the other planted firmly on the ground sat Creed. A beer was in his hand and he appeared relaxed and rock star like.

"Creed!" Chet called out over the noise and Creed turned his gaze toward us.

Chet stopped in front of their table and Creed stood up. "Hey," he replied, his gaze shifting from Chet to me lingering a moment then he nodded his head toward the table. "Have a seat."

The guy with the ponytail stood up and waved his hand for us to move inside.

"This is Dalm," Creed said by way of introducing us. "You met Jazz already and then that's Wayne."

"Thanks for letting us crash your table," Chet told them.

"We don't use it much anyway. At least you all can keep the others away," Jazz said with a shrug of her bare shoulder. The red halter top and tiny black leather wrapped around her waist to make a skirt was still all she had on. Most of her skin was exposed, and I was freezing just looking at her.

Chet slid in first then Griff motioned for me to go next. I liked the idea of being safely between Chet and Griff and went in quickly before he changed his mind.

"I'm Chet," he told the others then nodded his head to me. "Sailor and Griff."

Jazz smirked and reached for her drink. It looked like a tall glass of ice water. She said nothing though. I had been expecting something with the way she cut her gaze in our direction. It was probably best she remained silent. I didn't picture her as the polite type.

"I don't mean to interrupt but can I have your autograph?" a brunette asked, drawing everyone's attention in her direction. She was petite, curvy and very large breasted. She had dressed to make sure everyone saw just how big her boobs were. The girl was also only interested in Creed's autograph. She wasn't looking at anyone else.

"You are interrupting," Jazz drawled.

The girl blushed and glanced at her. "I'm sorry. I just really wanted Creed's autograph. I know when the set is over he will be covered by fans." She batted her eyelashes at him then.

"Got a pen?" he asked her.

She held out a black permanent marker to him.

"Paper?"

She shook her head and leaned closer and pointed at her cleavage. "Anywhere in this area," she said.

This time I was the one blushing.

"Oh give me a break," Jazz said and Wayne chuckled.

"I'll sign those big titties too, love," Dalm told her and winked. He had an accent, but I wasn't sure where it was from.

The girl acted as if she hadn't heard him. I found it interesting that she just wanted Creed's autograph when he was the new addition to the band. He couldn't have played many sets with them. He'd just moved in with Chet.

"I heard you play at Ringers this summer with Clayton. It was amazing," the girl gushed. I realized then that Creed had a fan base outside of this band. And had she meant Clayton Moore? As in the country singer who opened for my dad on last year's tour? Creed had played with him? I didn't picture Creed playing or singing country music.

Creed gave her a delicious grin and she almost melted on the spot and then he signed her right boob. Ewww. That was just trashy or maybe I was a prude. I looked away from them and scanned the packed bar. I was still completely aware of the conversation going on around me. I couldn't redirect my hearing like I could my vision.

"OHMYGOD! You're Sailor Copeland! OHMYGOD!" The high pitched tone the girl had taken made me wince. The noise wasn't as bad as the fact she was about to make a scene. I hated when this happened. I didn't live a life interesting enough for the tabloids and the pictures they did post were always surrounded by lies. Then there were the photos of me at the CMA's, Dad's Grand Ole Opry induction and other events. It was enough to make my face recognizable to a country music fan.

I forced a tight smile and looked at the girl, but before I said anything, Creed spoke up. "She's a dead ringer for sure but she's not that lucky. Hell, she's sitting at a college bar in Boston," he chuckled, as if the idea of me being here was funny.

The girl didn't look convinced. "Wow," she finally said still studying me. "I swear you look just like her."

I didn't speak for fear she'd hear my accent and the lie Creed had told would be blown. Instead I smiled and shrugged. The girl kept standing there, looking at me and it was Jazz who said, "You got your autograph. Bye," in a rude tone. I wasn't a fan of Jazz, but at that moment, I owed her.

The girl blushed and nodded then hurried away. I felt a little sorry for her but I was still thankful she was gone. The other eyes at the table turned to me and I could feel each curious stare. Damn.

"So, you're fucking Denver Copeland's daughter," Wayne said with a touch of amusement in his voice. Then he turned his attention to Creed. "Did you know that? You covered for her fast. Why didn't you tell us?"

I felt the panic slam into my chest at the realization that Creed had just unintentionally revealed he knew me...before three days ago. We'd lied. I'd lied to Griff. Why had I lied? I hated lying.

"I recognized her when I met her. I knew her name. Clayton bragged about touring with her dad all the time and Sailor was mentioned. I saw pictures of her with her dad online," he shrugged. "She wasn't telling anyone who her dad was so I figured she was keeping it a secret."

He was a much better liar and although that bothered me, the relief his lie brought me made it easier to breathe again. His words sank in and I wondered if he had looked me up online to see me now. Had he followed my dad's career curious about me? I didn't want to like that thought but I did.

"Thanks for the save," Griff said when I didn't. "She doesn't like attention from fans. You thought quick."

Creed didn't look at Griff, but at me, then gave a small nod before standing up. I wanted to thank him too but it felt like more of a lie. He'd just lied to them all and I didn't like being a part of it. I should come clean, but if I did, then I had to explain why I didn't tell Griff to begin with. My lies were beginning to compound.

six

OCTOBER 27, 2019
BOSTON MASSACHUSETTS

The bed was empty once again when I opened my eyes. Sunlight peeking through the curtains and cold air freezing my nose. I cuddled deeper into the covers and closed my eyes. Last night had started off tense, but after the band took the stage, I enjoyed myself. They were excellent and Griff danced with me.

The only time I had needed a moment to regroup was when Creed sang a song that he'd written that the band was playing. Hearing his much deeper voice sing again brought back emotions that I had thought were long since buried. I had to deal with that. Luckily we left shortly after because Griff said he needed to get in bed. Today he had a full day of studying but he'd promised that maybe we could go to dinner tonight and do some more sight-seeing.

I was in no hurry to get out of the warmth of the bed. I knew Griff and Chet would be deep in their books and that would leave me to converse with Creed. Somehow I felt raw inside where he was concerned. As if a bandage had been ripped off last night and the wound was still underneath. Facing that took more guts than I had. The sooner I got out of this place and headed to Portsmouth, the better. Next time I came to visit I would make sure Creed had moved out.

I heard the rumble of voices from the living room. If they were talking then Creed was in there. The other two wouldn't speak while they were studying. Griff was determined to make an A in Gross Anatomy. He'd always been an excellent student, making my GPA look weak. I was proud of his intelligence though and didn't feel like I was competing with him. He was the med student. Not me.

I was hoping the movers would call today with an update. Reaching for my cell phone, I turned the ringer back on and shivered. The warmth of the fire was what got me out of bed and wrapped up warmly in Griff's fleece robe and my fuzzy socks. The voices had quieted as I reached the door and I waited a moment to make sure things were silent in there before opening the door and letting the warmth of the room embrace me. I sighed and hurried toward the fireplace.

A masculine chuckle made me glance back without thinking because it wasn't Griff's. No, he was deep in is reading and hadn't noticed me sprinting across the room to the fire. It was Creed. He was leaning against the door to the kitchen with a cup of coffee in his hand, looking perfectly tousled. It was unfair that he woke up looking like a coffee commercial. I wanted to roll my eyes but didn't. I still felt as if I owed him for last night.

I managed a smile and turned back to the fire. My frozen body however was now forgotten. My thoughts were on Creed again, watching him play, hearing him sing, and wondering if he had followed my dad's career to see if I was pictured. It was a little narcissistic of me to assume that, that would be why he kept up with my dad's social media. Now I wanted to roll my eyes at myself. God, please let the movers call me today and magically be in Portsmouth.

"You want to make pancakes and bacon with the groceries you bought or should I go out and pickup breakfast?" Creed asked. I glanced back at him again. He was still leaning and looking perfect.

"I can cook," I told him, not wanting to go into the kitchen with him in there. I did buy the groceries to cook and I doubted they'd do any cooking when I was gone. No need to waste the things I had purchased.

"Want me to do the bacon and you make the pancakes?" he offered.

I started to say I would do both but I didn't get a chance.

"Definitely let her do the pancakes. She makes them light and fluffy. She can burn bacon like a pro though," Griff said and I jerked my gaze to him.

He smirked at my scowl. "I didn't fall in love with your bacon cooking skills, babe."

No longer wanting to stand near the fire for warmth, I headed to the kitchen while he laughed softly behind me. He was right of course. I had burned more bacon than I had gotten correct. It was a struggle to be sure. I just couldn't gauge when it was ready to take out of the skillet correctly.

"I would have thought you could cook bacon," Creed said as I walked past him into the kitchen. I gave him a sideways glance, not sure what he meant by that but I didn't ask. I went to the fridge and began getting out the things I needed for pancakes when I felt him come up too close for comfort behind me.

"Your Gran taught you to cook at a young age. Did she leave bacon out of the lessons?" He asked it in such a low voice that I didn't have to worry that Griff could hear him.

"Gran was a vegan. Remember?" I told him, taking the milk from the fridge then grabbing the butter.

"That's right. I'd forgotten." The way his tone changed caught my attention and I turned around to look at him. It was an odd change in mood. I bet he'd forgotten a lot about our summers. I didn't want to know just how much he had let slip from his memories. Not that I should care. It was best he didn't care. We weren't the same people that we had been back then. Our lives were very different and I had Griff. Creed caring would complicate things.

I stepped to the side and walked past him to set the items on the counter. "I was a kid so vegan didn't register with me. That mac and cheese she made us that was incredible was vegan?" he asked.

Looking at Creed made it hard for me to concentrate. I chose to keep my focus on making pancakes. "Yes. Everything she made was vegan."

"Damn," he muttered. "I dated a vegan once and the stuff she cooked tasted like shit."

I lifted my shoulders with a shrug. "It takes talent to make something taste good without milk, cheese, eggs, or meat." Which I knew firsthand. I had tried going vegan once two years ago. After a month, I found myself in Darryl's Barbecue, inhaling a pulled pork sandwich like a starving woman.

I heard him open the fridge door and assumed he was getting the bacon. I could have gotten it for him but I was too busy being awkward and uncomfortable. There was no reason to be. I was letting my childhood feelings for him get in the way. They were haunting me and I had to get control over them. We were adults now and that was a long time ago.

He didn't say anything more until I was flipping the second pancake. The bacon was filling the apartment with its delicious aroma and I'd relaxed some.

"Did you come back that next summer?" he asked me out of the blue. I hadn't expected that question. I just shook my head no. I didn't get into the reason why I didn't return was because he had shut me out.

"I spent it in London with my mom. I wasn't sure," he said.

I still said nothing. There was nothing to say.

"What did you do that summer?" he asked then and I wished he'd stop this. Talking about the past was not good for my head space.

"I stayed in Nashville for the most part. Dad was on a world tour and I met up with him in Sydney, Australia, then went with him to Melbourne and the Gold Coast before flying back home." I left out that the only reason I went back home was because Dad had met step-mom number two in the Gold Coast. She'd been twenty-three and obviously Australian.

"We let Cora down, you know. Not hiking the AT." His words surprised me. I'd not expected him to talk about Cora or the plans we had once shared. It was unsettling and sad at the same time. I wanted to remember her but I was afraid of the pain that came with that.

"I guess we did," was all I could say in return. My throat felt tight and talking was not easy.

"I'm starving, is it done?" Chet asked from the kitchen door. I hadn't heard him approach but then my thoughts had been elsewhere.

"Bacon is," Creed told him, before walking out of the kitchen. I fought the urge to watch him go.

"You can take the two pancakes I've finished," I said, attempting to sound casual and not like I wanted to cry.

He was right. Cora expected us to be together. We had been anything but together after the moment we found her.

seven

OCTOBER 28, 2019

I finished packing up the small suitcase with my things and then straightened up the bed and picked up the clothing Griff had left lying on the floor last night. He had left early for class, and I needed to get ready to head north.

Stepping into the living room with my suitcase, my gaze went to the chair where Creed was sitting. His left ankle resting on his right knee with a book open in his lap. I didn't remember Creed being a big reader, but I had seen him in this position often the past few days.

"You leaving?" he asked with a slight frown between his brows.

"Yep. Movers arrive today," I said, rolling the suitcase behind me and heading toward the kitchen for coffee.

"Is Griff not going with you?" he asked.

"He has classes. Besides the movers will carry everything inside."

He didn't say anything more and I was relieved. I sat my suitcase by the door then went to pour my coffee. When I turned around, I found Creed watching me. It made me feel self-conscious. I wondered if he would still be living here the next time I visited. I hadn't asked him how long he was staying, but I didn't think I needed to know.

"He could have missed a class to get you moved in," Creed said, looking aggravated.

I shrugged. "He is in med school. I hear that's hard," I said, trying to lighten the mood. I didn't not want to care that Creed was worried about me. I was blocking that out. I needed to get out of this apartment and away from him.

I drank the coffee in a few gulps, and luckily, it had cooled enough it didn't scald my throat. "Well, I am out of here. See ya around, maybe," I added with a smile and headed for the door. My escape.

Creed didn't say bye.

PORTSMOUTH, NEW HAMPSHIRE

Nothing had changed, but everything was different. I stood inside the house that had once been the only place that felt like home. It lacked the one person to make it complete. My Gran was my home and she wasn't here. Tears stung my eyes and I thought I had cried all my tears for her but seeing her things again brought it all back. What I had lost the day she died.

My boxes were all over the place, and I knew I would have to go through her things and make room for mine but I couldn't do that right now. I needed to be surrounded by her to get through this day and possibly the next week.

When the movers had called yesterday to let me know they would, in fact, arrive this morning to unload the truck, I'd been so relieved I hadn't thought about how this would feel. I had just been thankful to get away from Creed. He was my past and letting him dredge up the memories was bad for me.

However, I hadn't realized until last night that Griff wasn't going to be able to come with me or even come visit until next week. I knew he had classes and his studies were intense, but Portsmouth was only an hour drive. I had expected him to make a few hours for me and I'd been prepared to wait until he could come with me today. He had apologized about not having time today and said he would make it by the weekend to help me.

It wasn't unpacking I had needed help with, it was walking in the front door of Gran's with her gone. Explaining that to him was unfair. He had classes and he was a med student. I got that. I didn't want to be a needy female. When Creed has asked me why Griff wasn't coming with me today, I resented him for making me think about it.

Even after all the months the house had sat empty, it still smelled of Gran. Vanilla and cinnamon had always wafted through her house. She baked so much that she even smelled of vanilla and cinnamon. I loved that smell. She was the only security I had as a child and that scent was comforting to me.

"I'm back, Gran. To stay. Just like I used to tell you I wanted to do when I grew up. Except you're not here. You were supposed to be here," I said the words aloud and smiled even as a tear escaped and rolled down my cheek. I often wondered how someone like my mother came from Gran. They were so completely opposite. I mentioned it once to Gran as I got older and she said that Oliver, my grandfather, had spoiled my mother. They had tried for years to get pregnant and Gran had miscarried so many times they had given up hope. Then she got pregnant with my mother and from the moment my grandfather held her in his arms, he spoiled her.

Gran had then frowned and said that Oliver treating her like a princess had ruined her. I had to agree with that because my mother did, in fact, think she was a princess. I had never met anyone as self-centered as my mother. If I hadn't demanded she come up here for Gran's funeral and threaten never to speak to her again if she didn't then Mom wouldn't have returned from Paris in time.

I didn't want to think about my mother right now. I had other emotions to get control over. Walking through the house, I looked in each room and inhaled the scent of home. How had I thought I could live anywhere else? It felt right here as if being in this house fixed any problems in the world. I would finally get to have Christmas in this house. As a child, I had yearned to spend Christmas here with Gran…and with the Sullivans.

Stopping at the kitchen window I could see the neighbor's house. In the summer, it had been harder to see the Sullivan house from Gran's because of all the green leaves and plants. However, most of now colorful leaves had fallen and there was a clear view to the Georgian style house that had been built in 1778. It was still a pale yellow. The new owners hadn't changed the color. Except for the lack of a basketball goal outside it looked the same. Eventually I would go introduce myself, but I wasn't ready to see someone else in the Sullivans' home. The memories there were many.

While the Sullivans' Georgian style home was three stories and impressive in size, my Gran's house was smaller. My new home was a simple two-story colonial blue Greek Revival built in 1856. Downstairs was the kitchen, living room, dining room, and a laundry room with a toilet in it. Upstairs was two bedrooms and two bathrooms. The master bedroom had an en-suite; the second bedroom that had been my mother's then mine was larger but the bathroom was in the hallway at the top of the stairs. There was a small attic at the very top, but it was small. The house had a front-gable roof so that left only a small triangle of space up there.

Heating was going to be interesting. There was a fireplace in the living room and master bedroom and a wood-burning stove in the kitchen. That was it. No more heat. No central heating and air. The summers here had never been unbearable without the air conditioning I was used to in Nashville. Gran had always left all the windows up and box fans going in the most used rooms of the house. I'd loved it. I wasn't sure how I was going to love not having a furnace.

First thing I needed to do was find wood or I would freeze soon. Gran's woodshed was only a third of the way full, and I knew that she had needed a full shed. In the back of the house, there was a rack that also held a cord of wood that stayed close to her back door. Every August before I left to go home, Gran had already had wood delivered and filled up all her storage for the winter. When I had asked her why, she told me the cold came quick here.

I wrapped my arms around my body and shivered as I walked upstairs. She was right. The cold was here. I had almost had the movers put my things in my old bedroom, but then I decided I would need the fireplace in Gran's this winter. I headed to her bedroom at the end of the hallway and paused at the doorway to her room. The same blue and white quilt and white iron bed stood in the center of the room. The fireplace was in front of it, and there was wood already stacked to the side of it neatly in the holder.

Several pictures of me through the years sat on her mantel and one of my mother. The rocking chair where she had rocked me to sleep when I was little sat to the left of her bed, beside the nightstand with a crotched throw hanging over the back. It was as if she had never left. Her things still the way she would have kept them.

My suitcase and at least ten boxes worth of my clothing, shoes, beauty supplies and more lined the right wall. I would have to go through Gran's closet and pack her things up. The small attic she rarely used was about to be full. Tears were starting to clog my throat again when a knock on the front door startled me.

I turned and hurried back to the stairs, not sure who would be coming to see me. No one knew me really, not anymore. I reached the front door and opened it just after they knocked again. The face that greeted me brought a smile to my face. I hadn't been expecting this.

"Well, it's true. Sailor Copeland has returned to Portsmouth," Jack Tate said smiling at me. He had most definitely changed. His beard almost threw me off, but when he spoke, I was sure it was Jack.

"Jack!" I blurted out. "You grew up!"

He laughed at my stupid comment. "Didn't we all?"

I nodded. "Yes, we did. How are you?"

"Great. Married with a two-year-old. Can you believe that shit?" He chuckled then added, "Got a call saying you might need firewood. It's late in the season to get seasoned wood that don't cost a fucking fortune, but I can hook you up with three cords for $800. It's the family special price. I'll even stack it for you."

"That would be amazing. Thank you so much but let me pay you the going rate please. I was just about to figure out where and how to get firewood so you are saving me time and keeping me from freezing to death," I told him.

He shook his head. "Not a chance. You pay me $800 and that's firm. Just don't tell anyone. I don't give the family rate out often."

"Come inside, let me get my purse," I said, so relieved and grateful I might cry again.

"It's fucking cold in this house," he said as he stepped in the front door. "You got some wood out there. Why no fire?"

I picked up my purse and took my wallet out, before looking back at him sheepishly. "Uh, I was going to get to that."

He looked me over then and noticed my coat, gloves and scarf. "Sailor, do you know how to start a fire?"

I took out eight one hundred dollar bills then pressed my lips together in a tight smile. "Not exactly," I admitted. "I was going to Google it."

"Google? Fucking hell. Come on, girl. Let's go get some wood and warm this place up."

47

He took the bills from me and stuck them in his back pocket without counting them. I followed behind him as he headed for the woodshed. He began to tell me how to get kindling and wood then we went back inside so he could teach me how to start a fire. He did the one in the living room then he had me do the one in the bedroom while he watched. I was so happy with my success; I clapped my hands like a kid in a candy store. The wood burning stove in the kitchen was easier than I thought.

After he had told me all the steps I needed to do to keep the fire going, he headed for the door. "I'll be back in a truck before four. Me and my guys will stack the shed and the backdoor cord. Here's my number if you have any issues. Creed would never forgive me if I let you freeze."

That name caused me to pause as I reached for the card he was holding out to me with his number on it. "Creed?" I asked.

He gave a nod. "Yeah. Creed. Who'd you think called me to get me over here and set you up with wood?"

I said nothing, and he just smiled. "Glad you're back, Sailor. Hated seeing Bee's house sit empty. She'd love knowing you're here."

I nodded and I think muttered another thanks before he walked out the door and closed it. I stood there staring down at the business card in my hand. Creed had called him. My chest tightened and I hated the emotion I didn't want to acknowledge. Why did Creed care if I froze to death? I wanted him to not care. Didn't I?

eight

OCTOBER 31, 2019

This was Gran's house and my moving in was going to be a slow process. I needed time before I moved her things to put mine in their place. Instead of unpacking my boxes, I went out to buy pumpkins, carve the pumpkins, decorate the front stoop with said jack-o- lanterns, take pictures of it all and roast the seeds. Apple cider had been made using Gran's recipe from her recipe rolodex that sat on her kitchen counter. I had also made apple pie, candy apples, and pumpkin bread. All vegan of course. Luckily the health food store in town had the vegan butter Gran had listed in the recipes.

    Candy filled a black cauldron I had found in the attic along with a witch's hat, orange lights and a large fake spider and its web. My front door was now lit up and festive. I was ready for trick-or-treaters. This was a first for me. My mother didn't take me trick-or-treating when I was a kid. She thought the idea of going to people's houses to "beg" for candy was ridiculous. It was obvious my Gran did not agree.

The living room fire and the wood burning stove were keeping the downstairs warm, but I was still wearing a Vanderbilt hoodie and a pair of black leggings with fur-lined boots in the house. A "Spooky Tunes" CD I had found in the Halloween decorations was laying on the CD player Gran kept in the living room underneath the television.

I was winning Halloween this year. Gran would be proud. Picking up a candy apple, I went to go sit on the front stoop and watch the street prepare for the night when my phone rang. Taking my phone from my hoodie pocket, I saw it was Griff and a smile spread across my face. He had been busy studying for an exam this week and I hadn't heard from him in two days. He'd sent a few texts but nothing more. Tomorrow night he was coming to stay for the weekend. I couldn't wait. His lack of communication was worth it, knowing I would get to be with him soon.

"Happy Halloween!" I said cheerfully into the phone.

"Since when do you celebrate Halloween?" he asked with an amused tone.

"Since three days ago. My Gran did it up good every year it seems, so I am doing the same. I even carved pumpkins and roasted seeds. That is not as easy as it sounds either," I said, thinking about my first disastrous attempt at carving a jack-o-lantern.

"I take it you're giving out candy too," he replied.

"Oh yes! I also have candy apples to give out. My Gran's recipe."

He laughed and the sound made me happy. I loved his laugh. "Sounds like you have been busy."

"Very. I've made apple cider and apple pie, oh, and I'm wearing a witch hat to give out candy! I found it with Gran's Halloween things."

"I hate I will miss all that," Griff said.

"I'll save you some of everything for this weekend. I can even wear the hat for you if you want," I teased. "You are going to love this place. I had forgotten how magical Portsmouth is."

There was a pause on the line and I wondered if I had said something wrong.

"About this weekend. Sailor, I have a paper on medical ethics due and the one I had originally written I let Chet read. He thinks it's too weak, and he's right. I wasn't focused enough writing it. I need more research behind it. I just, I can't come this weekend, babe. I am so sorry. This paper is very important."

My festive mood was zapped just like that. All week, I had been thinking about seeing Griff and showing him Portsmouth and having him here at Gran's. We had barely had time to talk or he had barely had time. My schedule was wide open. I was also very alone here, and I missed him.

"You can't work on it here? There's a second bedroom that you can lock yourself away in and work." I just wanted him here. Didn't matter if I saw much of him.

He sighed. "I wish I could. I need the library resources here. Besides, the travel there and back is just more time that I won't have to work on this paper."

It was only an hour I wanted to point out but didn't. He was set on this. I knew that. I could hear it in his voice. I resigned myself to the fact this was going to happen. He was in medical school. "When do you think you can come?" I asked him.

"Next weekend. I promise. I'll be sure to have it all done and I will be free to spend every minute with you."

"Next weekend," I agreed.

We said our I love yous and byes then hung up. I started to put the candy apple down but decided I needed it. Grabbing a fleece throw from the sofa, I headed outside to sit and try and get back in the Halloween spirit.

I had just gotten wrapped up and seated when I saw the neighbors' front door across the street open. Six years ago, the Thompsons lived there, but I wasn't sure if they still did. Then I watched as Margie Thompson walked down the front three steps of her Greek Revival home, similar to Gran's in everything but color, proving that they were, indeed, still living there.

I watched Margie cross the road, carrying something in her hands, and realized then she was headed for me. Gran had been friends with the Thompsons. Their sons were about ten or more years older than me. I barely remember seeing them when I was growing up. When Margie was close enough, I could see she had a pie in her hands and a big smile on her face. I stood up as she walked down my driveway.

"It is so good to see this house lit up and alive again," she said as she reached the bottom of my stoop.

"Hello Mrs. Thompson," I said. It was nice to see they were still there. At least that hadn't changed.

"It's Margie. You're all grown up now. Here, I made you a Marlborough Pie. Now it isn't vegan like your Gran made, but it is delicious. I promise."

I took the pie and thanked her. She then waved a hand at the decorations. "Bee would be so proud of this. Just seeing the smoke coming from the chimney makes my days brighter. It is good to have you back, Sailor."

"Thank you, Margie," I said. "It's good to be back. It's not the same without Gran, but it still feels like home."

Margie nodded her head. "And it is! This is your home. This house has belonged to a Hobbs since it was built in 1856. The bloodline must live on here."

"Thank you," I said, not sure what else to say to that.

"Henry is coming over to wrap your outdoor faucets later and he's called Mike at the tire shop to come get your car and get snow tires put on. When Creed called Henry yesterday to ask him to help you get those things done, I thought how kind that boy still is. We are happy to help. Henry is retired now and he has nothing to do unless Dan brings his kids over for us to watch."

Creed again. The warmth in my chest came as if on command.

"Creed asked you?" I had heard her but I wanted to clarify. She nodded. "Of course he did. Fine young man he's become. Now, I have to get back home and prepare for my two grandbabies to visit before they go trick-or-treating. You call if you need anything. Come on over and knock whatever."

"Thank you, I will," I told her.

I watched her leave while holding the pie in one hand and my candy apple in the other, trying not to feel anything where Creed was concerned. Why was he doing this? Was this his attempt at trying to mend our past and be friends.

If only it were possible to just be friends with Creed Sullivan.

nine

NOVEMBER 3, 2019

Last night had felt several hours longer than just the extra hour that Daylight Savings Time added. The weekend itself had been tedious and lonely. I'd started out by going out to find trees still full of color and take photos, but they were all looking more bare than beautiful. I had given up and moved back indoors.

I worked on getting Gran's clothing boxed up, well most of it. I kept a few warm sweaters to use. They reminded me of Gran and this weekend, I had needed the comfort. My clothing was now all put away in its new home. I had also managed to unpack some of my picture frames and set them about. I put the photos of myself that Gran had sitting all over the place away and replaced them with pictures I had framed. Those of me and Griff, some of just Griff, two I had of me and Gran, one of me and Dad last summer, and the only picture I had with Mom in the past ten years.

It was starting to look a little more like I lived here. Putting all of Gran's things away didn't feel right. I wanted her things around me. It was as if a piece of her was still here. I put several of my boxes in the attic, not needing those things right now. There were less boxes sitting about and I felt accomplished.

Determined to enjoy my day, I made some homemade hot cocoa that I found in Gran's rolodex and sat down in front of my impressive fire to watch a Christmas movie. The Hallmark Channel was already full force Christmas and Halloween was barely over. I wasn't complaining, though I needed some cheer.

Griff hadn't called me all weekend. He'd sent one text yesterday asking how I was and after I responded in a three-paragraph text, he only said "Good" and that was it. I found it insulting, but I had to remind myself he was busy with his studies. I ate more Marlborough pie to soothe my feelings.

Today would be a good day. I was going to make it one. I was also going to look for a job online after I stopped being holly and jolly on the sofa. Sipping my hot cocoa, I decided if I didn't love meat so much, I could be a Vegan. The soy milk half and half I used to make the cocoa was surprisingly delicious. I could easily make Gran's recipes non-vegan, but something about making it exactly the way she made it felt nice. It helped the ache I felt when I saw something that brought back a memory of my time with her. Which was daily since I was living in her house now.

Just as the girl who was forced home to the blueberry farm to save the family business…had to leave her big city life in New York…bumps into the local restaurant owner who lost his wife to cancer several years ago…and is raising his daughter all alone, there was a knock on my door. I hoped no one else was bringing me a pie because I was going to have to run three extra miles a day after eating so much of the Marlborough pie Margie gave me.

I threw back the cozy red afghan that was keeping my legs warm and stood with my cocoa to go to the door. I tried peeking out the window, but it was hard to see who was in front of it from that angle. It wasn't as if someone in Portsmouth was going to be dangerous. Especially on this street. I opened the door, preparing to force a smile and do pleasantries with some friend of Gran's who was glad I was here, when a forced smile wasn't required after all. My jaw slightly dropped in surprise before I regained my composure and asked, "What are you doing here, Creed?"

The corner of his too perfect mouth lifted at the corner and he shrugged. "Had to come handle some business and thought I'd check on you."

I stood there staring at him, not sure if I was supposed to say thank you or I was fine or invite him in for cocoa.

He glanced up toward the chimney. "Looks like you got the fire figured out."

I nodded. "Thanks to Jack, which I should thank you for."

"I didn't want you to freeze."

"Thanks," I said again because I was still processing that Creed was here. Seeing him in Boston was one thing but seeing him at Gran's was different. Memories came back strong and emotions that I thought were gone rose to the surface and I had to adjust. Quickly before he noticed.

I shivered then from the freezing temps outside and stepped back into the warmth. "Come in and have some cocoa. It's cold out there."

He looked as if he wasn't sure that was a good idea and I concurred, but I owed him for helping me out with so many things I hadn't thought about. When he finally stepped forward and into the house, I closed the door behind him.

"Mrs. Thompson brought me Marlborough pie if you're hungry," I told him.

He shrugged out of his coat and hung it on the coatrack. "Sounds good. Thanks," he replied, and I hurried to the kitchen to get him the pie and cocoa so that I had a moment to get myself together and act normal. The way he made me feel felt like I was cheating on Griff, even though I had done nothing wrong. Facing my former emotions and overcoming them would be the smart thing to do. This was normal. It had to be. We had no real closure and I had battled depression that took me through too many dark days after Cora died and Creed exited my life.

"Christmas movies already?" he asked, walking into the kitchen from the living room.

I felt myself blush at being caught watching them but decided that was the least of my problems. "Yep," I replied. "How are things in Boston?" I then asked, feeling as if that was safe conversation territory.

"Same." His voice was close now. I turned to see he'd stopped only a few feet behind me. "Chet and Griff are either at school or studying. The food has dwindled in the apartment and when I checked for something to eat this morning, all we had was strawberry jelly, one egg, a quarter of a gallon of milk, and some leftover pizza."

"Yum. Nothing like jelly and pizza for breakfast," I replied, putting a slice of pie on one of Gran's everyday gold butterfly dishes.

"I wouldn't know. I stopped at Dunkin' on my way here."

Once I had his cup of cocoa ready, I picked up the plate and cup to turn and hand it to him. "This will be better than Dunkin'," I assured him.

He took both from me and I waved a hand toward the living room. "It's warmer in there. I haven't started the stove in here yet today," I explained.

I followed him back into the living room and picked my cocoa back up then went to the overstuffed tan chair, leaving him the sofa where he would have the side table to put his food and drink on. This was all very nice and friendly. I had nothing to worry about. It seemed we could do this. Besides, Creed lived in Boston. Not Portsmouth. I doubted we would have another visit in Gran's living room.

"What business did you have to take care of here?" I asked him, just to make conversation and a little out of curiosity.

He shrugged then swallowed his bite of pie. "Getting the wood stacked at the house, having the furnace serviced, that kind of thing."

Confused at his response, I waited until he took a drink and another bite then asked, "Your mom's house?" I would have thought her husband could do those things. What kind of man had she married? I remembered Creed's dad being handy around the house and making Creed help.

"No not mom's, my house."

His house? I let that sink in then sipped more of my cocoa. Why did Creed have a house here? Was he not moving to Boston? He was in a band there.

"The house I grew up in was given to my dad from his parents. The will states it can't be sold; it has to be passed down to the next in line. When my parents divorced, and moved out, Dad had the deed changed to my name. I've been leasing it to a nice older couple for the past five years, but they moved to Florida to be near their daughter who just had her first kid. I decided not to lease it again."

So…Creed was my neighbor? What?

"What about Boston and the band?" I asked him, not sure I was understanding correctly and hoping I was completely confused. For reasons, I didn't want to think too deeply about.

He finished his pie and set the plate down. "That was temporary. I was going to make it work with the distance if I enjoyed it, but it wasn't for me. I have only one more gig with them next weekend and then I move back here and finish what I started in college."

"College?" I blurted out without thinking. My head was spinning and I was struggling to make sense of all this new information.

He smirked. "What? Did you think I skipped out on college to play in a band?"

I had no idea that he went to college or where he went or if he had a degree. He had shut me out six years ago. He'd lost his sister, his twin, and I understood that he was hurting but so was I. There had been no reason for him to act as if I no longer existed. He had told me he loved me and after that I lost my virginity to Creed Sullivan. Four days later, we found Cora, dead. It had all changed. He didn't love me enough.

I wasn't that girl now. I was stronger. I had to be. Creed Sullivan had destroyed me once. That was something he would never have the power to do again. Griff loved me and he'd never hurt me like that. No matter what happened.

Remembering he had asked me a question, I got out of my head and replied, "I wasn't sure."

He didn't offer to tell me either. Instead he stood up, leaving his cup beside the plate on the table. "Thanks for the pie and cocoa. I'm glad you're settling in okay," he said. "I need to get some things accomplished before it gets dark, which will be fucking early today."

I jumped up as he went to the door and opened it. "Bye," I blurted out because there were so many things I wanted to ask and so many reasons I needed to just let him leave.

He gave me a single nod then left, closing the door firmly behind him.

I still didn't know what he had gone to college for or what he was doing back in Portsmouth.

Ten

NOVEMBER 5, 2019

I straightened my skirt, buttoned my navy wool coat, and wrapped a scarf around my neck before walking toward the entrance of The Islet at Portsmouth. I'd managed to get an interview on my first attempt to contact them. The Islet at Portsmouth was an art museum that was well-known in New England. To say I was nervous would be an understatement. Other than my degree and a short internship at the art museum in Nashville, I had little experience. However, the lady I had spoken to on the phone yesterday didn't seem to mind any of that. It was very likely they were going to hire me to run errands for them. I would take what I could get. Even if it was being a coffee girl.

The heavy door wasn't made of glass but oak and I would guess it was two hundred years old. Just the weight of it made the place feel intimidating. This was what I loved. It was what I had put all my time and effort into during my four years at Vanderbilt. I could remember my dad taking me to Musee

Picasso in Paris when I was nine years old. He was on a world tour, and my mother had stuck me on a plane to stay with him for two weeks of his tour. Anyway, that day had been the beginning for me. I loved every piece of art there and I wanted to study it and soak it in. I wanted more than anything to be able to create art like that but I wasn't talented with a brush or pen. I was good with a camera, but it wasn't the same.

I had left the Musee Picasso knowing, one day, when I had a job, I wanted to be surrounded by art. Now, here I was and my heart was pounding in my chest at the idea of getting to do just that. Stepping inside the museum, I let myself relax in the beauty surrounding me. I felt at home here. I always did with art.

"You must be Sailor Copeland," a voice said rather loudly from behind me. I spun around to see a woman, no taller than five feet, walking my way. "I'm Ambre Dupont Smith and although most of my name is perfectly French, I am not. My mother was born in Nice, France, but she came to the states as an exchange student, married my father who is a rancher in Wyoming and here I am. Now, you will need to assist Albert. That will be your title Assistant Archivist. Sign this paper and I will do a background check to make sure you aren't a criminal and then you can start. Albert will decide after one week if you are right for the job. He is not easy to work with but he is the best. Keep that in mind when you want to jump out of the top window to get a break from him."

I didn't notice the tiny woman take a breath while she said all of that. It was as if she'd said this speech a lot. It seemed memorized and her tone was as if it was tedious to repeat it all. I wondered how many times she had said it. Was Albert so hard to work under that this job was one that remained available? I was positive I could put up with anyone if I was Assistant Archivist. I hadn't expected a position that amazing. I could deal with a moody or difficult Albert, if it meant I was able to work with the art so closely. I'd tolerated my mother most of my life. She'd prepared me to cohabitate with insanity.

I signed the paper and she snatched it back up. "Very good. Come with me," she said and spun on her bright yellow pumps. Even though the heels on her shoes were short, they still provided height. It was possible Ambre Dupont was only 4 feet 10 inches. "Albert won't talk to you much. He rarely speaks. Pay attention to when he does say something because he won't repeat it. If you ask him to," she paused and glanced back over her shoulder at me and gave me a pointed stare over her oval turquoise framed glasses, "you'll regret it." She finished then stopped and opened another antique wooden door and walked inside.

"Albert, I have your new assistant. Please try and not run this one off. She's attractive and will do well for our events. We need an appealing face other than your own for the guests. Play nice," she said to the back of a dark bald head.

Albert remained with his back to us as he worked on a piece in front of him. His shoulders were wide and he was extremely tall. Albert looked more like a lineman in the NFL than an Archivist. He cleared his throat then turned around slowly. His gaze went from my face to my feet and back up again quickly before he frowned. I understood why Ambre had mentioned his attractive appearance. He was tall, dark and handsome. Clichéd but true. His eyes were the color of caramel and his lashes were so thick it was as if they were false.

"She's young," he said, shifting his intimidating stare to Ambre.

"Yes and maybe that's what we need. The older experienced ones leave because you're an ass," Ambre told him, giving him her own glare. He towered over the small woman in size, but she didn't seem to care. How scary could he be if this tiny woman wasn't afraid to talk back to him.

He looked annoyed. "They weren't meant to work with art. Had nothing to do with me."

Ambre placed a hand on her hip. "Yes, it has everything to do with you. Please try and work with Sailor. Don't send her running away until we see what she can do."

He looked unimpressed with her words and with me when he turned back around to continue cleaning the sculpture behind him. I only caught a glimpse of it, but I recognized it immediately. I'd seen it in photos but never in person. Once, it was supposed to come with an exhibit to Nashville, but it hadn't happened. I was so disappointed.

"La Sconfitta," I breathed in reverence at the beauty. "May I come closer?" I asked, my eyes locked on the sculpture.

Albert shifted his body so that the sculpture was in my view. "You know the La Sconfitta," he said not really asking.

"Crafted from marble by Andino after the defeat of his land," I said softly, as if my voice could harm the beauty in front of me.

"She knows her art. That's a positive. Don't send her away or I'm calling Katrina. She's tired of your late nights working due to not having help. If I must call your wife to come straighten you out I will," Ambre said firmly then spun on her heel and headed out the door.

Albert said nothing while I studied the sculpture. If seeing pieces like this one meant putting up with a moody man, then I would. He could do his worst. I wasn't leaving. I'd just scored my dream job.

"Why do you want this job?" he asked me brusquely.

I turned to look up at him and held my shoulders back and my head high. "There is nothing I love more than art."

He said nothing but made a sound close to a grunt then went to a large wooden crate that was unopened. "Loving art isn't enough. There must be a respect that is greater than even the love."

He handed me a screw driver. "Get the box opened."

That was my first order of the day and I was giddy.

eleven

Albert was demanding, rude at times, and not the best conversationalist; however, the man was a breeze compared to living in a house with my mother. I was made for this job. Walking to my car after nine hours in a room of priceless art, crates, and the aroma of coffee, I wanted nothing more than to call Griff and tell him about everything.

I stopped on the sidewalk and sent a text. "I got a job at an art museum! Can you talk?" Then I continued heading for my car. I was anxious for him to respond, but by the time I reached my car, he still hadn't. I slipped my phone into my purse. He was probably studying and had his phone silenced. Glancing down the street, I considered going to eat somewhere. I could order a cocktail and celebrate my new job.

"Sailor," a deep familiar voice called my name. I gripped the door handle on my car tightly, before turning to see Creed walking in my direction. He wasn't alone. A blonde woman was with him. She was gorgeous and tall. Typical Creed, it would seem. I waited until they reached me forcing a smile.

"Hello," I said, looking from Creed to the woman.

If my smile was forced, hers was completely fake. I wanted to tell her to cool herself. I was no reason to be jealous. He had several other females and she was not his one and only. Getting in my car and speeding toward home was now my goal. Forget celebrating. I'd break open some wine at the house.

"Headed home?" he asked me.

Yes, now I was thanks to him and Barbie. I nodded. "Just left work."

His eyebrows shot up. "You got a job already?"

My smile was no longer forced. Thoughts of my job made me smile and although blondie was giving me the stink eye now, I wanted to share the good news with someone. "Yes! The Islet at Portsmouth. I am assistant archivist." I felt pride in my chest saying the words.

Creed looked pleased. "Congratulations," he said. "Are you going to celebrate?"

I was but not the way I had planned. When I didn't respond right away he continued. "Let's go get drinks. It's on me. Stormie mentioned wanting a martini from Luciandas. We were headed that way. Join us."

Stormie did not want me joining them. It was all over her face. It was not my job to tell Creed he was with a potential psycho, but I was tempted to push her just enough that she cracked. The negative energy was not what I wanted surrounding me tonight. I much preferred my glass of wine at home alone. Hopefully talking to my boyfriend on the phone.

"Thanks but I'm expecting a call from Griff soon. I need to get home. Y'all enjoy your drinks," I said with the sweetest smile I could muster and flashed it at Stormie before opening my car door.

"Did she say y'all?" I heard Stormie ask, not even trying to whisper.

Creed said nothing and I closed my door before more words could be spoken and cranked it up ready for some heat. With a final wave at the couple, I pulled onto the street and headed for home. Nothing was going to ruin the elation of joy I was floating on. Especially not evil Barbie.

My cell phone rang, and my mother's name appeared on the screen in my car telling me who was calling. Not who I wanted to talk to right now. I started to reach forward and touch decline but decided getting this call over with now was better than her continuing to call until I answered.

"Hello," I said feeling no enthusiasm at all.

"Are you frozen yet? Ready to move back south?" she asked.

"I'm keeping warm. Gran has fireplaces and I have plenty of wood."

Mother laughed. "You can light a fire in a fireplace? Seriously, Sailor. It's a fabulous seventy-three degrees here today and sunny."

I was very serious and annoyed that mom would assume a fire would shut me down. Did she not know me better than that? No. She didn't. She barely knew me at all. "Where are you these days? California?"

"You know I'm talking about home," she replied.

Home. That was an interesting word. I never thought of the mansion I grew up in as a home. It was a showcase not a home. A place where nannies took care of me and my parents visited me. Nothing more.

"I just got a job at an art museum," I told her, not bothering to give her details. She wouldn't want them.

"Good luck getting to a job when the blizzards hit and you're snowed in for weeks. It's a frozen tundra there. I ran away as quickly as I could. I can't imagine why anyone would want to live in the Northeast. You have everything you could want here including art museums."

I wasn't sure why my mother wanted me in Nashville. It wasn't as if we spent time together. I rarely saw her. She jetsetted all over the world with her new man or friends. My being there or here should not affect her at all. The woman did not miss me. I knew that much.

"I like frozen tundras," I replied simply.

I could feel her rolling her eyes. "You know nothing of the cold there."

I knew I felt at home again since the last summer I spent with Gran. I didn't say that because I learned a long time ago telling my mother the truth led to her having a complete ranting meltdown. She preferred the lies in which she spun for herself. I preferred to keep her happy and to keep my distance.

"I'm almost at the house. I need to get the fire going and fix myself some dinner," I told her, in hopes of ending this conversation.

"Very well, go pretend to enjoy the cold," she said. "Kiss kiss," she added then hung up the phone.

Esma "Honey" Hobbs Copeland Muldoon never said "bye" or "I love you" when ending a call and she always hung up first. I was just thankful she had hung up.

Pulling into the driveway, I pulled under the small carport big enough for only one vehicle, but I knew I was going to be very thankful for it when the snow came. The house was going to be cold, and I grabbed the metal bucket beside the woodshed and filled it up before heading for the back door of the house. When I did things like this, it made me think of Gran doing these things. I'd never been here to see her in the winter, but I knew she'd done the same daily tasks. She would be happy to know I was here now doing them. The thought of that made the conversation with my mother seem unimportant. This was where I belonged.

Pulling out the key to the house, I unlocked the door and picked the wood bucket up then went inside. It wasn't as cold as I had feared, but it was chilly. I kept my coat on while I went to work heating things up. Once the kitchen stove was going, I stood in front of it while I opened the bottle of wine and poured myself a glass.

I was still standing in front of the warmth when I poured myself a second glass then picked up an apple from the bowl on the table and took a bite. I hadn't stopped for lunch today, and I wasn't hungry, but the wine was getting to me. I wanted to be on time for work in the morning and not hungover. I would need more than an apple for that.

I was almost warm enough to take off my coat when I finished my second glass of wine. Moving from the kitchen stove to the living room, I poked at the fire in the fireplace and then went to hang up my coat and scarf. Glancing over at my phone, I saw I hadn't missed a call or text. Frowning, I decided I'd drink one more glass of wine with a turkey sandwich. No need to let Griff being too busy get me down.

The simple task of making a sandwich and cutting up a cucumber for my dinner made me smile again. Either it was that or the wine. I wasn't sure. I poured another glass then went to sit beside the stove. The warmth felt wonderful. I could easily drink enough so that I wouldn't miss Griff.

Today had been too good to let Griff being busy get me down. He'd call when he had a chance. He always did. I worried he wasn't eating properly with all his studying and considered going to visit him just to buy some groceries. I wanted to see him too of course. He hadn't invited me to visit whenever I wanted though. That reminder made me sad again, and with a sigh, I picked up my sandwich.

Just before I took a bite, there was a knock at my door. Frowning, I set my sandwich down and looked at the front door. Who the heck was here this late? Getting back up, I went to open it.

Creed stood there on the front stoop. His leather coat zipped closed and his right hand tucked into the pocket while his other hand held a paper bag. "Hey," I said, unsure of his reason for being here and seriously hoping he hadn't brought Stormie.

He held up the bag. "I brought wine," he said, as if that explained everything. I glanced around for any sign of the blonde.

"Stormie?" I asked, not wanting to invite him in and have her pop out of the dark to follow.

"She needed to get home," he replied.

I stepped back then and let him inside. Once he was in the house, I closed the door quickly to keep any more heat from escaping. "I've already opened a bottle of wine if you want a glass," I told him and headed toward the kitchen. Seeing my sandwich on the table reminded me of my meal. "Are you hungry? I didn't cook but I have sandwich supplies."

I heard a low chuckle. "I'm good for now," he said, as he took the bottle of wine he brought out of the bag and placed it on the bar.

I sat back down in the chair beside the fire and took a sip from my glass.

"Glasses?" he asked me and I realized I had been in a hurry to get warm I had forgotten about getting him a glass for his wine.

"Sorry," I said and pointed at the cabinet directly across from him. "In there."

He got his glass and walked over to the table to sit down and pour himself a glass from the open bottle in front of me. "Tell me about your job," he said, leaning back in the chair. He hadn't taken his coat off. I was about to offer to take it but figured he knew where the coatrack was, so he must still be warming up.

I finished the bite of sandwich in my mouth then beamed at the chance to talk about my new job with someone who wanted to listen. "It's perfect. I didn't expect to get such an amazing position when I went in this morning. I thought I was interviewing for a job that would be more along the lines of errand girl. I have a degree, but my list of qualifications stops there. This is my first real job. Anyway, lucky for me, the reason the position was available and they were willing to interview someone with such limited experience is because the Archivist, Albert, isn't the easiest guy to work under. They can't keep an assistant for him. He runs them off. However, Albert has nothing on Honey. I was raised to deal with difficult. Besides Albert isn't that bad. He's demanding, sure, and you better listen when he speaks because if you don't hear him the first time, you're screwed. He doesn't like being asked to repeat himself."

I stopped to take a drink of my wine and Creed looked like he was enjoying his glass as well as my description of my new job. So I continued.

"Today he was uncrating a new exhibit from Italy. There were pieces I had studied but never seen, except one. I saw it when I went to visit my father in Rome one time. I knew the pieces and my knowledge and art nerdiness finally paid off. Albert warmed to me before the day was over. He didn't have to tell me names of the artwork or go into detail over how to uncrate them. We worked well together in the silence. I felt like I was in a dream most of the day."

I finally stopped and just smiled at how ridiculous I must sound to someone who wasn't obsessed with art the way I was.

Creed set his glass down and leaned forward, resting his elbows on the table. "Albert would be an idiot to lose you. I'm happy you got your dream job. Especially here in Portsmouth. Your Gran would be proud of you."

I hadn't thought about that. Gran would be thrilled over my new job. She would have made me a massive dinner complete with vegan mac and cheese. Tears stung my eyes at the thought, and I blinked them back. It was embarrassing to cry over something like that now.

"I'm sure Griff is happy you found a job you love so quickly," Creed said, reminding me that I had a boyfriend who still hadn't texted or called me back.

Frowning, I picked up my wine and took another drink. I was sharing my good news and celebrating over drinks with Creed. Not Griff. This wasn't how it was supposed to be. I set my glass back down onto the table gently and lifted my gaze to meet Creed's. "Yeah, he's thrilled," I said, instead of admitting he hadn't called me back yet.

Creed lifted the almost empty bottle of wine. "Want the last little bit? I can open the bottle I brought."

As tempting as drinking my sadness away over Griff not calling was, I shook my head no. "I have had too much already. You can have it."

He didn't question that and poured the rest into his glass. It was so odd seeing him at Gran's table; yet at the same time, we had sat here hundreds of times before. We had been kids excited for her cookies, we had been awkward preteens unable to stop looking at each other, and we had been teens in love determined to spend every moment we had of the summer together. Our history was deep, and although that meant something, there was still the darkness at the end. The pain came with it. Now he was here and I didn't know why.

"Why did you come back, Creed?" I asked him. I hadn't the last time he stopped by, but now I wanted to know.

"While I finish up my Master's in Architecture, I am lucky enough to be working with a group of architects that are restoring the Frontsman Lighthouse, just off the coast in Portsmouth."

That was not what I was expecting but then it made sense. Architecture fit Creed. He'd always been interested in old buildings and the history in New England.

"That sounds amazing," I told him.

He nodded. "It's pretty damn cool."

"I thought you were going to be in Boston this week," I said, remembering he had told me as much Sunday when he stopped by.

He shrugged. "Things came up here and I reworked my schedule."

We sat there a moment and I wanted to ask him more questions. I wanted to know all about how he decided on architecture. I enjoyed having him here. I enjoyed it all too much. A warning bell went off in my head. This could lead to nothing good. I was missing Griff and I didn't need to fill that void with Creed.

"I've got an early morning tomorrow and I want to do some reading on the exhibit we are working on. I have to stay ahead of Albert and not let him intimidate me." That was the truth. I needed to do both those things but I also needed Creed out of my Gran's house. Having him here messed with my head in ways I didn't want it messed with. Creed was my past.

He didn't question it. Instead, he stood up and finished his glass of wine then walked over and set it in the sink. "You keep the bottle I brought. Might need it after another day with Albert tomorrow," he said then winked at me.

I stood up and followed him to the living room. "Thanks for coming. I didn't want to be alone after all it seems," I told him.

He turned back to look at me with his hand on the doorknob. "I wanted to hear about your job and you gave me a good reason to send Stormie home," he said with a smirk. "Goodnight, Sailor Moon," he added then opened the door and stepped outside.

He hadn't called me Sailor Moon since I was sixteen years old. The emotions that came with that memory were so strong I found it difficult to respond. Words clogged in my throat along with the lump that had formed. He wasn't the only one who had called me Sailor Moon. Cora had called me that too when she was teasing me about her brother. Those memories were bittersweet and it had been a long time since I let them in.

"Goodnight," I managed to say.

He gave me a nod and headed into the darkness toward his silver Jeep.

twelve

NOVEMBER 7, 2019

It took Griff twenty-four hours and three minutes to call me back. He apologized profusely saying he had a test to study for and then spent the next ten minutes telling me about his class, the questions on the test, how important it was, and in the end, the grade he'd made. When he was done, he'd forgotten about my new job and asked me what I had been up to.

I knew he was burdened with classes and making the grade, so I overlooked it and repeated the fact I had gotten a job and told him about it. However, it wasn't until we hung up after a less than fifteen-minute conversation that I realized I hadn't gone into detail about Albert or the exhibit the way I had with Creed. I didn't want it to bother me but it did.

Creed had more time and he didn't have the weight of med school on his shoulders. I couldn't compare his desire to listen to me ramble on about my new job to the limited time that Griff had. That wasn't fair. Just like it wasn't fair for me to ask Griff when he would be here to spend the weekend.

He didn't mention it and I didn't ask. Which meant he wasn't coming. I could tell by the tone of his voice and the way he was talking about needing to write a paper that he had no time to come up here to see me. I wouldn't let that get to me. Albert had informed me we'd be closed on the weekends during the next four months, except for a couple weekends in December when Portsmouth had another round of tourists. I would come up with something else to do over the weekend. Maybe I should clean. I also had a few boxes left to unpack.

Today was Thursday, though, and I wouldn't worry about that now. Besides, Griff may still call this evening or tomorrow with plans of coming to visit. I could also go visit him. Tonight I would open up the wine that Creed had brought me the other night and watch Hallmark Christmas movies. No thoughts of Griff or going to see him. That could wait. Today had been a great one at work and we had almost unfinished uncrating the exhibit. I was excited about the coming week when we would prepare for opening the exhibit to the public.

When I pulled into my driveway, a silver Jeep was already parked there and the engine was running. Exhaust from the heater gave that away. I parked under the carport and wrapped my scarf around my neck, before opening the car door and stepping out. Creed was already out of his Jeep standing in front of it, waiting on me.

"Hey," I said more pleased than I should be to see him. It was hard to get lonely when he kept showing up.

"Come with me," he said with a grin on his face. I wasn't sure any female would say no to Creed Sullivan when he told them to come with him. So, I didn't feel guilty when I nodded and asked no questions before heading to the passenger side of his Jeep.

When we were both inside the warmth I buckled up the looked at him. "Where are we going?" I asked him.

"Do you remember Fleur Young?" he asked me.

How could I forget? Fleur was in love with Creed when we were kids. One summer when I had returned, they were an item although it didn't last. My returning to Portsmouth had ended it quickly. Creed had broken up with Fleur and we had begun our whatever it was when we were fifteen. Fleur tried to make my life hell when she got the chance.

"Uh, yes. I recall Fleur," I said the words a little too sourly.

Creed chuckled and I cut my eyes at him. "It's been awhile but I don't think Fleur wants to rehash old times with me. We have no old times worth speaking of," I told him.

His crooked grin was so damn sexy I had to look away from him. Why did the man have to get better with age? He had been beautiful enough when we were teenagers. Just ask freaking Fleur Young about it.

"Fleur and her husband, Josh Clark, own a bar in Hampton. It's not a big place, but it's on the water and they have the best Lobster rolls in the state. Some nights they have live music. I fill in for them if I can. Just me without a band."

Fleur was married. I relaxed a little then and I knew I was being ridiculous. I wasn't with Creed. If they had been dating that would have been fine. I wasn't sixteen anymore. Odd how my thinking it over rationally still didn't make the idea of Fleur and Creed together okay.

"Oh," I said, trying not to sound as happy about Fleur's marital status as I was.

"I'm going to play for two hours tonight. They don't stay open late this time of year. Not enough customers."

"Sounds nice and I've not had a lobster roll since I've been back in New England."

He shook his head. "Shame on you."

We rode in silence for a moment then I felt Creed glance over at me. "You weren't really going to hold our past with Fleur against her still, were you?"

I bit my bottom lip a moment because I wasn't sure if I was going to lie or tell the truth. A lie would save me the embarrassment. Finally I just said, "Old habits die hard."

Creed laughed loudly then and I smiled, liking that I'd made him laugh. Even if it was at me. He had a great laugh. It was something I used to love to hear and rarely did anymore.

"Derek is one of my friends now. I learned to forgive and forget," he said in a teasing tone.

Derek Clark was Fleur's brother. He was one year older than us, but I didn't recall a reason for us to dislike him. He had always been nice to me. "Derek was never an issue," I reminded him.

"Not to you he wasn't. He worshiped the ground you walked on. If you'd told him to jump off a cliff, he'd have done it and taken a fucking selfie in the process."

I turned my head to look at Creed. "No he would not! He was just a nice guy. He had to be because his sister was trying to make my life hell."

Creed rolled his eyes. "You were blind to poor Derek's efforts. If I hadn't been so damn jealous, I would have appreciated it more. I couldn't laugh about it back then because I was terrified you'd fall for the older, popular guy."

I frowned. Was he serious? I didn't recall Derek Clark having a thing for me at all. He was just a sweet guy. "I think you're remembering things wrong."

Creed raised his eyebrows then. "Okay. Then I'll ask Fleur about it tonight. We will see who is remembering things incorrectly."

The idea of asking Fleur about her brother's attraction to me six plus years ago made me cringe. I'd rather just say I was wrong now and forget about it. "That's okay, I believe you."

He chuckled and kept driving. I had a feeling he wasn't going to let this go. Before I could think of more reasons for him to forget about this, we were pulling into the parking lot of "On a Clark Shell." Okay, so that was a cute name for the bar.

"I don't play until seven thirty so we have forty minutes to eat. Can I trust you not to attack Fleur while I'm on stage?" He was teasing, but I still glowered at him then got out of the truck.

He was around the truck before I had the door closed. "It's a little icy," he said, then held out his arm for me to take. I looked down at his arm and thought about it for a second then decided I was thinking too hard about something so silly. Taking his arm, we walked toward the entrance, and twice, I almost slipped and would have busted my ass had he not being holding me up.

When we went inside, the warmth of the place was a relief. The closer to the water, the colder the wind it seemed. Outside felt frigid. There was a large fireplace that sat on the far-right wall and I wanted nothing more than to sit at a table near that. It looked toasty and the view to the stage in the center of the back wall would be perfect.

We were greeted before we could go too much farther by a young brunette in jeans and a black t-shirt that said *In a Clark Shell* on the front. "Good evening, Creed." She blushed as she said his name. "Where can I sit you tonight? The usual?" She couldn't be older than nineteen years old.

Creed looked down at me. "You want to sit near the fire, don't you?" he asked me.

I nodded. "Please."

He turned back to the waitress, "Lulu" or at least that's what it said on her name tag. "Tonight, let's try the booth by the fire," he told her.

She gave me a smirk as if I were a lightweight that needed heat then spun around to strut with an over-exaggerated swing in her hips toward the booth by the fire. I glanced at Creed and he didn't notice the extra effort Lulu was making. I felt a little bad for her but not completely. Creed was looking toward the stage then his eyes came back to me.

"Nice place, isn't it?" he asked.

I nodded. It was a nice place. I liked the cozy feel. It was very New England.

"Creed!" a female voice called out from across the restaurant.

We both turned to see a grown-up Fleur walking toward us. Her boobs were bigger and at sixteen, I didn't think that was possible. Her fiery long locks were a deeper auburn than they had once been. Her large round stomach sticking out like a basketball had been the most significant difference. Fleur Clark was pregnant. Creed had left that out.

She saw me and paused mid-step, and for a moment, I wondered if sixteen-year-old Fleur was about to take over but then she beamed at me and put her hands on her hips. "Oh my God! Sailor Copeland!" she said then continued her path toward us. "Creed Sullivan, you did not tell me you were bringing Sailor," she said as she reached us.

"I thought I'd surprise you," he said smiling smugly at me. I felt stupid for my attitude about Fleur in the car earlier. We were grown-ups now for goodness sake. I had been silly to think otherwise.

"Lulu get this woman whatever she wants. Don't let her cup get empty," she said to the blonde waitress then looked back at me. "I am thrilled you're here. It's been a lifetime ago it seems. When did you get back into town?"

It was as if there had never been issues between Fleur and me. She acted like any grown adult would with a childhood acquaintance. "Two weeks," I told her. "I moved into my Gran's house."

She swung her eyes to Creed then back to me. "Neighbors again," she laughed then. "The talk in Portsmouth has already started I bet. I'm surprised Derek hasn't called me and told me. He should be here tonight too. Have you seen him?"

I shook my head. I hadn't run into Derek in town and I didn't realize he still lived there. I wondered if he too had a spouse and offspring. She laughed then and cut her eyes back to Creed. "Competition is good for you. God knows you need some."

I wasn't sure what that meant, but Creed smirked. "Sailor's boyfriend is a med student in Boston. He's my cousin's roommate."

About Tomorrow...

Fleur's eyes went wider then she laughed out loud. "I need some entertainment in my life. Other than swollen ankles and not being able to see my feet anymore. God, I wish I stilled lived in Portsmouth."

Creed took my arm and motioned his head toward the booth. "Ignore her," he said with a roll of his eyes.

I moved into the booth so that when it was time, I could see the stage clearly. Creed moved into the bench across from me. "If you're done making up drama that doesn't exist, we'd like lobster rolls and I want and Impy Stout." He glanced at me. "What do you want to drink?"

I hadn't seen a drink menu and I wasn't one to know my order. I liked to see the specialty cocktails. However, if they didn't have one, I was afraid it would be rude to ask.

As if she had read my mind, a menu was placed in front of me by Fleur. "These are our specialties. I suggest the Hampton Falls. It's incredible if you like tart and sweet. If you prefer a smoother slightly sweet then the Snowy Sunrise is a great one."

I decided I'd try both. "I'll start with the Hampton Falls," I told her. Fleur appeared pleased.

"Keep the menu. You can try more," she told me then winked before turning and walking away rather impressively for someone that far along in her pregnancy. Wasn't she supposed to be waddling around by now?

"She's a real witch, isn't she?" Creed asked casually after she was far enough away she couldn't hear me.

I shot him a sheepish look. I already felt bad enough assuming she would still be mad at me for taking Creed away from her eight years ago. "She's great," I said honestly.

He leaned back and crossed his arms over his chest grinning. "You'll like Josh too. They're good people."

I was sure I would. "Did all our friends get married and start procreating?" I asked him.

He gave me a wry look. "Apparently most did. There are a few still living the single life. Fleur's brother Derek for starters.

He was engaged a couple years ago, but she left him for a divorced surgeon and moved to Manhattan. Greg Harris is still single, he was the curly haired kid that lived at the end of the street. A foot taller than everyone else and the goofball."

I had forgotten about Greg. He had lived to make people laugh back then.

"What about Ryan?" I asked, before I had time to think about what I was asking. Wincing, I started to apologize but Creed seemed okay with the question. Ryan had been Cora's boyfriend the summer she killed herself. She had crushed on him for years and that summer I had wondered why she didn't seem happier about finally getting him.

"He's not married either. He's had a hard time. His mother died of cancer two years after Cora died. His dad remarried and he didn't take it well then a year into that marriage, his dad decided to end his life." Creed stopped then and shook his head.

I didn't know what to say when Creed mentioned suicide. Losing Cora the way he had made it a sensitive subject. Causing him anymore pain wasn't something I wanted to do.

"Your beer." A waitress that looked older than Lulu appeared with our drinks. "And a Hampton Falls. Fleur got your orders in and food should be out shortly. I'm Mary, if you need anything," she said, before turning to head over to a table across the room.

Creed brought up a memory with Fleur and Derek that I'd forgotten. After that, we talked about funny things that had happened over the years with all our other friends in Portsmouth. Creed even spoke of Cora, without looking as if it was painful to remember her. We had finished our lobster rolls that had indeed been amazing and I was on my second drink the Snowy Sunrise when Creed had to leave me to go get set up on stage.

I wasn't there alone for long; Fleur came over and sat down beside me pulling up a chair. Either it was because she couldn't fit in the booth with her stomach or she wanted to see the stage.

"How has life been Sailor Copeland?" she asked me with a sincere smile. Fleur was happy. There was a glow about her that you couldn't fake.

I shrugged. "Good. I went to college in Nashville. Met my boyfriend there. Graduated then moved here to live close to Griff while he is in medical school."

She took a drink from a fancy bottle of water she was holding. "I saw you two years ago at the CMA's and I told my brother he needed to fly down to Nashville while you were still unmarried. That black dress you had on with those red boots. Fire!" she told me.

I smiled and thanked her, not sure what else to say about the mention of her brother. "Derek doesn't go after life the way Creed does. He isn't one to live spontaneously. He's too career-driven and focused," she sighed. "My brother is boring."

"Career-driven and focused is a good thing, I think. Griff is that way," I said then glanced over at the stage. "I think not knowing or understanding someone makes it harder to trust them."

Fleur didn't say anything just drank her water.

After a few moments, she rested the bottle on her knee. "I don't know. I think the guessing makes life fun. Too much focus can lead to dull and boring. My husband, Josh, I never know what that man is going to come up with next, but I trust him without question." She seemed so secure as she spoke of her husband. I was happy for her and a little envious. I missed Griff and having him near me. When we had been at Vanderbilt, we had spent every day together We had studied together or at least in the same room.

Now, he barely called, and I didn't even know what he was doing this weekend. He hadn't called to tell me. I missed him…I missed us.

"I'm glad Creed brought you. Last time he brought someone, she was annoying. Kept sending drinks back to the bar with complaints and our bartender is the best. If she hadn't been here with Creed, I'd have told her to leave. I did ask him not to bring her back."

I had seen some of the females Creed spent time with. I wasn't surprised.

"I'm glad he brought me. I love your place and it was good to see you."

She leaned forward and sat her bottle on the table. "Come back with or without Creed."

I nodded. "I plan to," I told her. "I'll bring Griff when he's in town."

Fleur smiled then stood up. "I need to go check on things in the back and make sure the lady at table five is happy with her special order."

I watched her go then turned to look back at the stage, just as Creed greeted the crowd and began to play. His eyes met mine as his he began to sing. A warmth that seemed to come with Creed Sullivan's gaze ran through me. I felt guilty as I shivered but I didn't look away. His deep voice was mesmerizing. The corner of his mouth lifted in a crooked grin as he continued to look at me.

It felt like we were the only people in the room. Although it was only eye contact the power of it excited…and scared me.

Thirteen

NOVEMBER 9, 2019

The weather wasn't going to get much warmer than it had been yesterday, although the weatherman said we would see a high of forty-one degrees. Yesterday, we never got over thirty-seven. I had called Griff twice yesterday and then left him a text before I went to bed. He still hadn't returned my call or text and it was eight thirty in the morning. I was going to assume he was not coming since it was Saturday and he'd not found time to call and tell me when to expect him.

I was snuggling under a heated blanket with a cup of coffee in one hand and the other tucked under the covers. I didn't see a reason I should leave the house today. I could clean, unpack the last two boxes, and order some thicker curtains for the bedroom. I had read that it helped keep the room warmer in cold months. Might as well try it.

My phone was beside me on the table when it began ringing at exactly eight forty-two. I sat my coffee down and picked it up seeing Griff's name on the screen. Excitement that I might be seeing him today took over and I jerked it up ready to hear the sound of his voice.

"Hello!" I said cheerfully into the phone.

"Hey, babe. Keeping warm?"

"I am currently in front of the fire under a heated blanket. And you?"

He chuckled. "Yeah. I'm sorry I didn't get back to you yesterday. Class went long then we headed to the library for some study material. By the time we were back in the apartment, I was too tired to do anything but eat a sandwich and crash. When I woke up on the sofa, it was too late to call you."

That made sense. I felt guilty for being mad at him yesterday for not at least texting me back. "It's okay. I hope you got some rest."

"I was up at four back on this paper." He paused, and I knew without him saying anymore that Griff was not coming today. I let the sting of disappointment come then I shoved it away. I was dating a man in med school. I had to adjust. "I don't think I can make it this weekend."

I almost said I would come there, but I knew he didn't need me as a distraction. He'd have asked if he wanted me there. "It's okay. I already figured you were busy." That was the best reassurance I could manage. I wanted to cry in my coffee and feel sorry for myself.

"I promise soon I will get up there. I miss you," he told me and I could hear the sincerity in his voice. This wasn't easy on him either.

"I miss you too," I told him.

"Talk soon, I love you," he said.

"I love you," I replied and then he hung up.

I pressed end and sat my phone back on the table then reached for my coffee. I had expected this, but it hurt nonetheless. Not only that but he hadn't asked me one thing about my job or life here. He was always short on time and I never got to tell him anything anymore. We used to talk about everything.

Tears filled my eyes and I let them fall. I needed a good cry and it wasn't hurting anyone for me to cry alone in my house. I missed Griff. I missed Gran. I missed having someone to tell things to. Griff wasn't just my boyfriend but my only friend. I didn't have many friends in Nashville, simply because I learned at a young age that no one wanted to be my friend. They wanted to be near me so they could be near my dad. To say they met someone famous. Even worse to slip him a CD of them singing or a song they wrote. I had stopped having friends a long time ago. When I had met Griff, he hadn't even known who Denver Copeland was and I had loved him for that.

Tomorrow I would get up and go grocery shopping and maybe go shop for Christmas decorations but right now, I was going to sit home and sulk. It was warm inside and I knew outside it was still freezing. Besides I was good at being alone. I'd been alone most of my life.

Cleaning house and unpacking the rest of my boxes had only been enough to keep me busy until lunch. I was now done with my egg and avocado sandwich. I had nothing to do. I stood in the kitchen, looking out the window at the people out in their yards. You would think it wasn't overcast and forty degrees. These folks had thick skin.

Deciding I needed to get out, I went to grab my fur-lined boots and then my heavy coat. At least I could go for a walk. I needed some exercise. I also needed to acclimate to this climate. Staying inside bundled up wasn't going to help with that. I was almost to my mail box at the end of the drive when a red truck slowed down in front of the house. It came to a complete stop and the driver side window rolled down.

"I thought Fleur was full of shit but damn if you don't look good, Sailor Copeland," Derek Young said, looking older but still handsome.

"Hello, Derek," I said smiling up at him. "It's good to see you."

"Creed's already taking you out I see. Didn't take him long," Derek replied.

I paused not sure how to respond to that.

"No it doesn't," Creed replied, and I spun around to see him walking across my yard heading our way.

Derek chuckled. "Like old times. Almost," he said and shook his head.

I felt like I should clarify that it was not like old times. Creed wasn't the love of my life and I had a boyfriend. I wasn't sure how to phrase that exactly and I didn't have to because Derek nodded his head at me. "See you around, Sailor." Then he rolled up his window and pulled back onto the road.

I turned back to Creed who was now standing beside me. "He thinks we're dating," I told him.

Creed shrugged. "Good."

'I frowned at him. "Good?"

He gave me a crooked grin. "Old habits die hard."

I wanted to be mad at him, but instead, I laughed. Today had been a crummy one so far and seeing Creed made it better. I wouldn't dig too deeply into that.

"Want to come see the place? I've had some remodeling done. Just started moving in today," he told me, nodding toward the house next door. His house. The Sullivan house. The last place I saw Cora alive. I wasn't sure I could go inside that house.

"Okay," I said instead. He was moving into that house again. He had good memories there and I understood that. I had good memories there too. Most of them had Cora in them. I wasn't sure I was prepared to face that after all this time. However, I wasn't going to tell him that. It seemed too difficult to express. We weren't close anymore. I didn't feel safe sharing my feelings to him as I once had. Especially when it was about Cora.

Creed began walking back toward his yard and I fell into step behind him. He didn't say much. I expected him to start talking about what he'd done or some kind of small talk. His mood had changed it seemed. I never knew which Creed I was going to get. It was unsettling.

When we reached the door to the house, he opened it and then motioned for me to go inside. I paused, wondering how this would affect me. Did he have a hard time walking back in after all these years? If Creed could live here, then I could walk inside I told myself and forced my feet to move forward. Still he said nothing.

It smelled the same. Gran's had smelled the same too, but then there had been no remodeling when I moved into her house. This house truly looked much different. The downstairs was brighter and more open. Less walls and closed-off rooms. The wall color was a simple white and the light fixtures were new and not the antique ones that had once been on the wall. The wooden floors had been worked on too, although I could tell they were still the original floors of the house. They didn't make them like this anymore.

Even with all the paint, sheetrock, polished floors, the house still smelled the same. Memories flooded me and I held them back the best I could. It was as if at any moment Cora would walk down the stairs smiling. I wondered if he'd changed anything on the next two floors.

"All I've done upstairs is repaint and have the floors refinished," he said when he saw my eyes go to the stairs.

"It's breathtaking," I told him honestly. I'd always loved this house. He'd just made it look like a different one downstairs. It had been traditional New England before, but even with its fresh new look, it was still a beautiful place. I didn't ask him why he changed things because I would have changed them too. Just so being here didn't feel like it had…before. Changing it would help with the memories or at least I hoped it did.

"Mom hates it. She said I messed up the history but," he paused. "I needed to."

"I understand," I said simply. Because I did. There was a lot I didn't understand about Creed Sullivan and I doubted I ever would. It was too late to try. But I understood his need for this place not to feel the same.

"I know," he replied.

I turned to look up at him and his gaze was already on me. We stood there like that for longer than necessary, but I couldn't look away. Words that had never been said hung there in the silence and I knew now I didn't need to know. I had desperately wanted him to talk to me six years ago and the idea of that happening now…terrified me.

fourteen

JUNE 3, 2013
PORTSMOUTH, NEW HAMPSHIRE

This wasn't how summer was supposed to be. Everything was different this year. I sat on Gran's back porch alone. Gran had gone to get groceries and I was too busy sulking to go with her. She'd promised me a cupcake from the bakery if I went as if I were a child. I wish a cupcake was all it took to make me feel better.

Cora had cheer camp this week and she'd be home next week. We would have the rest of the summer together and she'd texted me several times since she left. I was happy she made the team. That wasn't my problem, although it did make me sad that one of our weeks together this summer was gone.

I glanced over at the backyard of their house that I could barely see through all the trees and hydrangeas. Not that it mattered. No one was there. Creed had a girlfriend now. Fleur freaking Young. I didn't know her, but I knew she had Creed. He was barely around. With Cora gone and Creed with Fleur, I was without a Sullivan friend. This summer was turning out awful.

Footsteps on the gravel driveway caught my attention. I didn't see anyone yet and I wondered if I should go inside and lock the door. I was here alone and I wasn't expecting anyone. Before I could make a move, Creed appeared around the corner.

I stared at him.

"Hey," he said with the crooked smile I loved and wished I didn't. Before this summer, Creed had always been…well, mine. We hadn't been boyfriend and girlfriend or anything like that but he'd always been there. He was my Creed or he *had been* my Creed. Now he was Fleur Young's Creed. The thought soured my attitude more.

"Hi," I replied and turned my gaze away from him and back to the yard. I didn't say anything more and I didn't look at him, but I could see him from my peripheral vision and I knew he was coming closer. If Fleur Young came around that corner next I was going inside. No, I was sprinting inside.

"Want to go get an ice cream?" he asked when he reached the stairs I was sitting on.

I wasn't a kid. Did everyone around here still see me as a child? Gran trying to buy me a cupcake and now Creed offering ice cream. I bet he didn't take Fleur for ice cream. She probably got taken to the coffee house.

"No thanks," I replied, still not looking at him.

He sat down beside me on the steps and I wished he would just go. I didn't want to deal with him. He was the main reason I was in this terrible mood and having the worst summer ever.

"You're mad at me," he said.

Yes, I was mad at him, but I wasn't telling him that because then I would have to tell him the truth. I had some pride. I would not tell Creed Sullivan that I was almost positive that I was in love with him. He didn't need to know I counted down the days every year until I got to see him again. Even worse that when Chase had asked me to the homecoming dance, I had told him yes but just as friends because I had a boyfriend in New Hampshire. Which was a complete lie but I hadn't wanted Chase to think I was available to date. I didn't want to date anyone but Creed Sullivan.

"Tell me why you're avoiding me," Creed pleaded. I didn't want to be mad at him or avoid him. I just didn't know how to be around him and Fleur when I was sure I loved him.

"I'm not," I said, forcing a smile and flashing it at him. When I started to turn away from him again, he caught my chin with his fingers.

"I know you, Sailor Copeland, and you are avoiding me," he said, making me look into his eyes that were unfair to unleash on any female.

A lump formed in my throat and if I cried on him, I would have to leave Portsmouth. I could never face him again after that. I could not cry. I had to be cool. Like Fleur was cool. The thought of her made me want to roll my eyes, but I didn't.

"You've been busy," I said, and the thickness in my throat made my voice sound weird.

He raised an eyebrow. "When have I ever been too busy for you?" he asked me.

Now that he had a girlfriend. That's when. Jeez was he going to force me to spell this out for him? Because I didn't want to do that. Humiliation was not a strong enough word. I shrugged instead.

He tilted his head to the side and studied me. "Is this about Fleur?"

Ding, ding, ding! I remained still and silent. His fingers stayed on my chin and I couldn't look away unless I jerked my head and that was too dramatic.

"It is," he said then his hand left my face.

I felt instant sadness at his letting me go. Was the revelation that I was jealous of Fleur going to send him away now? Would this be the last time we talked all summer? Would my sulking lead to our friendship ending? I didn't want that but how did I stop it?

Creed rested his hand on his knee with his palm side up. I stared at it then back at him. He gave me a crooked grin and boy had I missed that grin. "I broke up with Fleur. She was taking up all my time and the truth was I just wanted to be with you."

"Oh," I replied in a whisper.

He nodded toward his hand. "You going to make me beg or are you going to give me your hand?"

"Oh," I replied again, still reeling at the news he wanted to be with me. He missed me too. I slowly slid my hand over his and his fingers laced through mine, before closing over my hand.

"Now, I really want a freaking ice cream. Would you come with me? Because I'm not letting go of your hand or you."

A giggle came from me before I could stop it. When had I become so silly and giddy from Creed's attention? "Okay," I said.

He stood up and I went with him, our hands still clasp. "You know I was only dating Fleur because you were dating that tall football player guy."

I paused confused. "What?"

He didn't look at me then but said, "Facebook. I saw your picture at the dance with him. Everyone commenting about you two being a cute couple."

"Chase?" I asked, realizing he'd seen that picture and assumed the wrong thing. I hadn't thought about Facebook. Someone else had posted that picture on my wall, not me.

He shrugged. "I don't know his name."

"Chase was not my boyfriend and we were not dating. We just went to the dance together."

He didn't look convinced. "People called you two a couple."

I shrugged this time. "They wanted us to be…I think Chase wanted us to be. I made it clear to him it was just as friends."

"You didn't like him?"

I didn't reply right away. I could say I didn't like Chase that way and leave it at that or I could be honest with Creed. He had been honest with me. This summer was different. We weren't kids anymore. I only had a couple of months with him.

"Chase is a friend. He's nice, but he isn't who I like. I told him there was someone else…in New Hampshire."

Creed looked down at me then and I could see the pleased look in his eyes. "Really?" he asked.

I nodded.

His lips broke into a full grin. "It's about damn time."

"What is?" I asked him, returning his smile.

"Us, Sailor. It's time for us. I've been waiting for what feels like forever."

fifteen

NOVEMBER 12, 2019
PORTSMOUTH, NEW HAMPSHIRE

When I pulled into my driveway around seven that night, it was nice to see the house next door lit up again. It had been dark at night since my arrival until two nights ago. Although I hadn't seen Creed since Saturday, when he gave me a tour of the house, I saw his lights. He was home and that made me feel warm inside. It was strange I know but it did. I liked knowing he was there.

I wondered if he was hungry and considered making a big pot of chili and calling to invite him over. Other than Albert at work, I hadn't talked to anyone in days and I was lonely. Albert couldn't be considered a conversationalist. Griff had texted twice to tell me he was busy and would call soon. He still hadn't called.

After parking the car, I walked toward Creed's house, deciding I'd invite him over for dinner if he hadn't already eaten. It was a neighborly and friendly thing to do. I didn't get very far though when I saw a brunette with long brown hair standing in the kitchen with a glass of wine in her hand laughing at something.

He had company and I was doubting he was hungry for food. Turning back around, I headed for my house and another night alone. I was getting good at dinner, the Hallmark Channel, and wine in the evenings. It wasn't a bad thing. Soon we'd have snow and I could have holiday parties by myself.

Sighing, I unlocked my door and went inside the cold house. Doing my regular routine, I hurried and got the fireplace going then moved to the wooden stove in the kitchen. I kept my coat on until things warmed up, but I found my furry slippers and took off my heels and put them on instead. Maybe I would get a puppy…no, those could be a lot of trouble and needed attention. I had work. Oh! I could get a cat. They liked being left alone for the most part.

Pouring myself a glass of wine, I went to the living room to turn on my trusty companion, the television, and then stood in front of the fire. I was almost warm enough to take off my coat when there was a knock on the door. I sat my empty wine glass on the coffee table and went to the door.

Creed was standing outside, holding a large pot with oven mittens on his hands. Was he bringing me dinner? "Hey," I said stepping back so he could come inside.

I glanced behind him, hoping the brunette wasn't about to follow him. I didn't see her. "Are you bringing me your left overs?" I asked.

"No, I'm bringing dinner over here to eat."

I looked outside again to make sure the other woman wasn't out there then closed the door before any more warmth escaped.

"Since you just got home, I figured you wouldn't have eaten yet," he said as he sat the pot on my stove.

I walked into the kitchen behind him. "Uh, no, I haven't eaten yet," I replied. "I was about to make some chili but I never made it that far. I've been warming up."

He leaned back against the counter and crossed his arms over his chest casually. "Good. How's your week going?"

He was staying? I looked out the kitchen window toward his house. "I uh, thought you had company?" I said, wondering why he was here with me holding a pot of something in his hands.

His eyebrows drew together in a slight frown then he smiled. "Are you talking about Rachel?" he asked.

I had no idea who I was talking about. I didn't know the woman I had seen through his window but then Creed had a lot of women it would seem. "I guess if that's the woman at your house."

He shook his head. "Rachel isn't company. She's family. Our mothers are first cousins and she's lived most of her life in London with her father. She just left her fiancé at the altar this weekend and fled to the states. I got a call yesterday from her, asking if I'd pick her up at the Boston airport. Somehow from that I got stuck with her hiding out at my house for now."

A female that he wasn't dating. I wasn't expecting that. "So you don't want her to stay?" I asked him, getting the feeling his coming over here made more sense now. He was getting away from his cousin.

"I like Rachel, in small doses. She's loud and bossy. She talks a lot about herself. I needed some peace. I brought dinner with me, hoping you'd let me stay," he said with a hopefulness in his tone that made me laugh.

"Sure. Who am I to turn away a warm meal. I'm exhausted from work and cooking didn't sound appealing."

He let out a dramatic sigh of relief and I laughed some more. Creed was grinning at me then he winked before turning back around to his pot of mystery meal. I was happy he was here. Not being alone was much better than my previous few nights.

"What are we eating?" I asked him as I took out another wine glass from the cabinet.

"Clam chowder," he replied.

"You can make clam chowder?" I asked impressed and unaware his culinary skills were so good.

He glanced over his shoulder at me. "No. But I can order takeout."

That made me laugh and he smiled again. I loved that smile. Wait. No. I didn't need to love anything about Creed Sullivan. That was wrong. Wasn't it? I shouldn't be loving something about another man unless he was related to me.

"Where's the bowls?" he asked, opening a cabinet that held my Gran's baking dishes.

"Here," I said, walking over to the other side of the stove and opening the correct cabinet for him.

I took out two bowls and handed them to him. "Did Rachel eat already?" I asked.

"Rachel doesn't eat. She drinks her calories or at least that is what she told me when I asked."

"Sounds like a health freak," I joked as I got us both a soup spoon and took them to the table.

"She's fucking nonstop female chatter. Do I look like I want to know when she starts her period or how bad her cramps are?"

I laughed out loud again then covered my mouth and shot him an apologetic look over my hand. He smirked and sat a bowl of chowder in front of me then set his down. "It's funny. I know," he said with a sigh and pulled out his chair to sit down.

My kitchen was small but cozy and with Creed there to give me conversation, it felt like home. We ate and he shared some more of Rachel's drama with me to make me laugh. He had no interest in her female problems, but he was using them to entertain me and I appreciated it. I needed to laugh. The chowder was delicious, and before I knew it, we had finished the entire bottle of wine.

When he stood up from the table, I thought he was about to leave and I didn't want him to go. Not yet. I liked having company and not feeling so lonely. "Do you want to watch a movie?" I asked, hoping that didn't sound desperate.

He put his bowl in the sink and turned back to me. "Yeah, I would," he replied.

I knew he was staying just to get a break from Rachel, but I would take whatever I could get. We moved to the living room and Creed went and sat on the sofa. I picked up the remote and glanced over at the chair.

"I don't bite. Besides I'm also warm," he said and patted the space beside him.

This was innocent and harmless. We were old friends and the idea of getting to snuggle to someone was so very appealing. I missed human contact. I didn't let myself think about it much longer and went over to sit down beside him.

Creed reached over me and took the blanket I had thrown over the side arm then covered both of us with it, before putting his arm on the back of the sofa and with his hand moving me against him by nudging my shoulder gently.

I inhaled deeply and he smelled amazing. He felt hard and he was right, warm. I wanted to sigh with pleasure of being near someone again and I refused to think it was because it was Creed that it felt so good. I was just affection deprived. That was all this was.

Creed took the remote from my hand when I did nothing with it to find a movie. He scanned the channels and settled on *Lost in Translation*. It was just coming on and I hadn't seen it in a while. Good choice. Although, I'd probably be happy with a horror flick if I got to watch it like this. I hadn't realized how much I missed being near someone else.

Creed began slowly stroking my upper arm and my eyes felt heavy. He chuckled at something happening on the movie and I soaked up the sound of his chest rumbling. I knew I was falling asleep and I wanted to enjoy this longer, but my eyes wouldn't stay open.

I woke up when Creed laid me down on my bed. Blinking slowly, I stared up at him. I didn't know how late it was or if he had finished the movie. "I'm sorry," I said groggily as he covered me up with all four of the blankets I kept on the bed.

"For what?" he asked in a low voice.

"Falling asleep," I said.

He smirked then and brushed some hair out of my face. "It was tough. I hate it when beautiful women snuggle up against me and fall asleep in my arms. but I'll forgive you."

Smiling, I closed my eyes unable to fight off the sleepiness.

"Goodnight, Sailor Moon." I heard him whisper and I must have fallen asleep again because I dreamed he kissed my head and then my cheek.

sixteen

NOVEMBER 13, 2019

My alarm went off and rudely woke me up. Yawning, I reached over and turned it off then stretched. On my second yawn and grumble about having to wake up, I smelled it. A fire. Sitting up, I stared at the fireplace in front of me and the fire roaring in it. What the heck? My room was warm as I tossed the covers off me and slipped on my house shoes. I was still wearing yesterday's clothes, a pair of stretchy slacks and a blue sweater.

Creed had put me in bed. I looked back at the fire and then headed for the door. Was Creed here? I hoped so because if Creed hadn't started the fire, I had a very thoughtful intruder that I hoped hadn't warmed me up to kill me.

Stopping at the top of the stairs, I heard the crackling of the fireplace downstairs and I smelled coffee. Slowly, I made my way down, almost convinced it was Creed but prepared if it wasn't. I should probably be armed, but I didn't think about grabbing a hairbrush to whack over someone's head before I started down the stairs.

When I reached the bottom step, I turned right into the living room and sighed with relief when Creed was sitting on the sofa with a cup of coffee in his hand watching the television. He turned to look at me and smiled. "I hope I didn't wake you starting the fire in your room."

"Uh, no, you didn't," I replied, not sure if it was rude to ask him why he was here or if he'd stayed all night.

He nodded a head toward the kitchen. "I made coffee."

Was it okay he had stayed the night? He obviously hadn't slept in my bed. The other side was untouched like it was every morning. We were friends. We'd slept in the same apartment in Boston. Griff was there though. We had been alone here, but it wasn't the same.

"I couldn't figure out how to lock your door without the key last night," he said.

"Ooooh," I replied, understanding dawning on me. "So you stayed? Please tell me you slept in the other bedroom and not on the sofa."

"Nothing was wrong with the sofa. It slept good."

I covered my face with my hand. "I am so sorry I fell asleep on you. Thank you for staying."

"Like I said last night I'll get over it," he replied then winked…again. He needed to stop winking. No man should look that good when he winks. It's not fair to females. Especially those of us who have boyfriends that they love.

"I'll make you breakfast," I told him, hoping I had time to do that and get a shower before I needed to leave.

"I'm good. Go get ready. I'll head back home," he said standing up. "Rachel will still be asleep, and I will have some peace until I leave work."

"I hope she doesn't hate me for keeping you all night," I said.

The right corner of his mouth lifted in a half-grin. "She won't. She thinks we are sleeping together," he replied, then opened the door and left without another word.

She thought what? I started to run after him but then glanced at the clock. I didn't have time for that conversation. Thanks to Creed I didn't need to build a fire in the kitchen stove to warm me up or make coffee. I grabbed a cup and headed upstairs to shower. Trying not to think about how much I enjoyed last night and snuggling up to Creed like a hussy was difficult but I did try.

Albert was oddly cheerful. It didn't mean he spoke more than three words at a time but he was still in a good mood. The exhibit was set up and tomorrow would be opening day for it, which meant tonight an elite crowd would attend a cocktail party to view it first. The guests would consist of patrons that helped fund the art museum. I'd helped address and mail all fifty-seven invitations that had gone out my first day on the job.

Today the museum had more life in it. The party planner gave out orders while the cleaning staff, caterer and decorator scurried to do her bidding.

It was a little after two when Albert said I could go home. We were to be back here by six and I would be expected to mingle and answer questions about the items in the exhibit. I was also told I could bring a plus one, but Griff had finally called me this morning on my drive to work to tell me he was sorry but he wasn't going to make it tonight but that he swore he'd come visit on Sunday. I doubted that and it made me feel guilty for being pessimistic. I'd wanted him to see my job and stand beside me at tonight's event. I was silly to get my hopes up that he would make it. He was stressed with his load at med school and I knew it was hard on him. I shouldn't have asked him to come.

By the time I was home, I'd convinced myself that it was best I didn't have a date. I needed to give my full attention to the guests tonight and answer all their questions. They were the reason the art museum existed and I was thankful for my job. I also loved talking about art and tonight I would get to do a lot of it. My thoughts were deep in everything I needed to remember for tonight that I missed the thin brunette coming across my yard and straight at me until I looked up to put the key in the door.

"Hello!" Rachel called out, raising her hand in greeting. Long red fingernails wiggled at me. Apparently, she wasn't mad at me about keeping Creed all night.

"Hello," I replied with a smile.

She reached me and put a hand on her curvy hip. "I'm out of shape," she said, taking a deep breath. "Anyway, I'm Rachel, Creed's cousin. I wanted to come introduce myself and be nosey. He told me about you and I remember Cora talking about the two of you when we were younger. She loved teasing him about you during the holidays, which was the only time we ever saw each other. I just hope you can get him to want more than sex. That man and his inability to have a real relationship is sad." She rolled her eyes as if exasperated.

What had Creed told her? Did she think we were sex buddies? And if so why would he tell her something like that? Couldn't we just be friends that didn't have sex? He had enough real sex buddies or whatever the many females he dated were called. Annoyance at Creed overcame the warm fuzzies I had been feeling about his staying last night and warming up the house for me.

"Oh, uh, yeah, well you know Creed," I finally replied after a pause. Why was I covering for his lies? I was, though, and I couldn't bring myself to tell her the truth. What was wrong with me? I needed therapy again. That was it.

"He's a good guy who loves women but you know that. You've been his Sailor Moon forever," she said with a bright smile. "Well, I'm headed to the spa. I need a massage and some relaxation. I'll see you around. We can do tea one afternoon," she said, looking excited about the idea. I didn't share in her excitement.

"Okay, yeah." I managed to agree as she turned and hurried back across the yard in her high heeled knee-high leather boots. Which I had to admit were kind of fabulous.

Opening my door, I went inside and realized then that I was frozen. It was below freezing today and I'd just been forced to stand out in it. Hurrying to the fireplace, I hoped it would light quickly. Sometimes it did and sometimes it didn't. Today was going to be one of those difficult days where I struggled and cursed the cold.

Just before I gave up and went to light the wooden stove in the kitchen, the fire took and I sighed in relief. I was tempted to go get my electric blanket and wrap it around me and my coat. First, though, I went to get my phone and sent my first text to Creed.

"Did you tell Rachel we were sex buddies?" I was getting angry again just thinking about it as I hit send. There was no reason to lie about something like that and it was embarrassing for me. I was not and would never be one of Creed Sullivan's many females. The idea was insulting.

"No. She assumed it. Why? Did she come visit?"

I read the text and immediately replied. "Why didn't you clarify the situation? Why let her think that?" Was he so desperate to get away from her, he couldn't take five minutes to tell her we were just friends? No sex involved.

My phone rang then and I saw Creed's name. Frustration about his lie and Griff not coming to the party tonight snowballed.

"You're an ass, Creed Sullivan. I do not want to be one of your many females. I don't like someone thinking that I would be okay as your fuck buddy. It's insulting. Do you have any idea how embarrassing it was to listen to your cousin tell me how she hoped we could evolve into more because of our history?" Okay, now I was fuming. The more I talked the louder I got.

"I didn't mean it that way. She asked who I was taking the chowder to and I told her it was you. She remembered Cora talking about you…and me before. She thought we were back together and I didn't want to give her your life details, so I said no, we were just friends. She assumed you were like my other female friends or fuck buddies as you call them. I didn't correct her. I just got out of the house. My staying the night didn't help. I will make sure she knows the truth. I'm sorry, Sailor."

That all made sense but I wasn't done being mad. I wasn't sure I was even mad at him anymore but I was just mad. "Fine! You do that!" I said too loudly then hung up. Staring at my phone, I burst into tears and threw it down on the sofa.

The tears started slow at first, then I was bent over in a full-blown bawl. I missed Griff. I missed being with him. I missed the fun we had together. I was almost positive he didn't miss me. He didn't act like he missed me and it hurt. I kept thinking we would get settled into a routine and be able to see each other more, but every day that passed that he didn't make it to see me, I began to fear we never would.

Backing up I sat down on the coffee table and held my head in my hands and cried until my tears dried up. All the pent up frustration, anger, anguish, and fear that I had been ignoring broke free. Missing what Griff and I had in Nashville, accepting the fact Creed was now back in my life, not feeling as if I belonged anywhere, it all had become too much. Pretending I was okay wasn't helping me. I had become a ball of emotion.

When I was done, I felt lighter. The anger was gone but the sadness was still there. It just had less power to control me. I'd let it out and I felt stronger.

I sat for a few more moments and did some breathing exercises I learned in counseling then wiped my face dry. I was going to be okay. Griff and I were going to be okay. This was a rough patch but it was life and we would get through it. I didn't think Griff was sitting around crying. He had too much studying for that. It was just me who was struggling. I was the one who needed to toughen up and get through it.

Standing back up, I made my way to the stairs to take another shower. It felt like I needed it to wash away the rest of the sorrow. Tonight, I would have a wonderful time doing what I loved to do. Nothing else was going to bring me down.

seventeen

A better choice in shoes would have been the only thing I would've changed about tonight. Smiling into my flute of champagne, I took a small taste and let Albert handle the questions for a moment. The museum was full of men dressed in tuxedos and women adorned with diamonds. The guests didn't intimidate me, although Ambre had seemed concerned earlier today that they would. Neither Ambre nor Albert knew who my father was, and even if I told them, I didn't think they'd be impressed. Neither of them appeared to be fans of country music.

I liked that about my job too. At work, I was myself, Sailor Copeland. Not Denver Copeland's daughter. In Nashville, I wasn't afforded that privacy. I had to deal with cameras going off in my face if I went out on a date and cameras going off that I didn't see when I did something as simple as swimming. Griff had been great about our first date being on the cover of a gossip magazine.

My eyes caught a couple standing over by the Custode Segreto, a painting of a young girl hidden partially behind a door. It left one wondering what it was she saw, what it was she was hiding from, or who it was she was hiding from. I loved the depth of darkness the artist had taken to bring you into the moment. Worried for the child. You didn't want her to get caught.

I set my flute on an empty tray and made my way over to the couple. The woman noticed me approaching first and her smile was genuine, unlike many I had encountered this evening. Not that it mattered. "Can I answer any questions you may have about The Custode Segreto?" I asked.

"What year was this painted? I don't recall seeing it when we visited this exhibit in Rome," the man replied.

"This was first displayed in eighteen thirty-six. It has only been with this exhibit for the past two years. Before then it belonged to a Mr. Chanade Nieler in his private museum within his home in Italy."

They seemed pleased with my answer.

"I'm going to get another drink," his wife informed him and excused herself.

When he seemed to have no more questions for me, I made my way over to stand away from the guests again. I didn't want to crowd them and the art was meant to be enjoyed. No need to stand in their way. I'd been lucky enough to help unpack almost every piece.

Ambre was beaming with pleasure as she walked toward me. The silver stiletto heels she was wearing tonight almost put her at eye level with me. If I hadn't been wearing heels they would have. "Excellent job tonight. I've heard only good things tonight about you. They seem to be pleased with you as does Albert. I can't think of the last time this place has ran so smoothly."

I didn't see how I helped that any but I smiled feeling pleased. "It's been a great event."

She nodded. "Yes, it has and the donations we've received have been more than enough to cover the cost of this exhibit.

They're all about to start slowly heading out. Go on and leave. No need for you to stand around until they're gone. Have a long weekend and we will see you Monday. Oh, and send me the photos you took of the exhibit and set up. I'd like to send them to the paper."

I started to offer to stay, but my feet reminded me that I was abusing them in my choice of heels. I promised to email her the pictures I'd taken then went to the back to get my purse, before slipping out the door without drawing any attention to myself. I paused when I got close enough to my car to see a dark figure leaning against the driver's side door. It was dark and whoever it was stood just outside the street light's glow. For a moment, I thought it was Griff, but then I realized how unrealistic that was. Griff was busy like always.

The figure moved into the light when I stopped walking and the glow illuminated Creed. I didn't start walking right away, mostly from confusion at his being beside my car. I hadn't thought it would be Creed. My surprise passed quickly and I realized I was happy to see him. I wanted to tell someone about tonight and Creed was here. I wasn't sure why he was here but he was and I could tell him all about the exhibit and the donations.

"Hey," I said, smiling when I reached him.

He didn't say anything at first and I remembered our earlier conversation. Was he mad at me now? Had he come to finish our argument? I had every right to get angry. I started to tell him just that but he spoke first.

"I'm sorry," he said.

He'd already apologized but then I hadn't been nice about it. "Thank you," I replied. "I was having an…emotional day, I guess, I shouldn't have gotten so angry."

"No, you were right. I spoke to Rachel. She knows that we are just friends."

"Thank you," I said again. My earlier outburst seemed silly now. Had it really mattered what his cousin, who lived in another country, thought of me? Was it my conflicting emotions making me over react?

"How was opening night of the exhibit?" he asked me.

I sighed from the memory of tonight. "Amazing," I told him. "I was able to talk about the art and people listened. They wanted to know all the details and I got to tell them. I love it."

"You look beautiful," he said, as his gaze slowly went down my body with an appreciative gleam.

The giddiness from my evening had to be the reason my stomach did a flip and my heart felt as if it was fluttering. I felt flushed suddenly and the night sky was my friend as it helped cover up my reaction to his words. I should thank him but I wasn't sure my voice wouldn't give away exactly what I was feeling.

"Griff should have been here with you," he said and my fluttery feeling turned sour. That wasn't his business and the way he had said it sounded as if he was judging Griff. He had no right to judge Griff.

"He is a med student," I stated the obvious. "An art exhibit isn't as important as his studies." I was annoyed and I didn't try and hide it.

"Anything that is important to you, should be important to him. He should have prepared and made time to be here. Not doing so was selfish."

"You don't get to say what he should and shouldn't do."

Creed took a step closer to me and his eyes blazed down at me. I wasn't sure if it was anger at me, at Griff, or at something else. "You fucking deserve for your boyfriend to be by your side when something as important as tonight happens. Does he know how much you love your job? Does he know about Albert and how you've charmed the moody bastard? What about the La Sconfitta and that you finally got to see it first hand? Does he know any of that, Sailor?"

Tears stung my eyes and I hated it. I didn't want to be emotional especially, not in front of Creed. This wasn't fair. He was making it sound like Griff didn't care and he did. He just hadn't had time...yet he was right that Griff knew none of those things. Creed did. It was Creed I had told all of that to. It was Creed that was there to listen. None of this was fair to Griff. He was working so hard.

"Come on," Creed said gently, taking my upper arm and leading me toward my car. "Let me drive."

I shook my head no. I didn't want him in the car with me. I wanted to be alone and I wanted to cry. He didn't let go of my arm as he led me around to the passenger side. "You've had a long day, it's late, and I've upset you. Let me drive you home."

He was right. It had been a long day and he had upset me. When he opened the car door, I climbed inside silently. There was no reason to argue. I wanted to be mad at him but it wasn't working. He had been right about a few things. He was the one there to listen to me. Griff hadn't had time, so I'd used Creed as a stand-in and he'd been such a good listener. He even remembered the name of the La Sconfitta.

I laid my head back on the seat and closed my eyes as he climbed in and started the car. I didn't want to need Creed or enjoy him being around. It scared me. I'd loved him as deeply as a girl could love a boy once. So deeply I'd needed counseling when he was suddenly gone from my life. But I wasn't a girl anymore. I was a woman and he wasn't the boy I'd adored. Letting him get too close was reminding me of how I felt before and it was wrong.

"I like Griff. He's a good guy," Creed said, breaking the silence.

I kept my eyes closed and said nothing. I didn't know what there was for me to say. I didn't trust myself to verbalize all I was feeling.

"I just want you to be happy, Sailor."

I opened my eyes then and turned my head to look at him. "What makes you think I'm not happy now?" I asked him defensively.

He let out a weary sigh and glanced at me then back at the road. "Because I know you. I know when you do that frown where the corner of your mouth turns down that whatever you're thinking about is making you sad. I know that when your eyes twinkle, you are trying not to laugh. I know that you scrunch your nose and shake your head when you don't want someone guessing the truth," he paused and looked at me again. "I fucking know you."

My eyes filled with unshed tears and when I blinked, a tear broke free and I quickly wiped it away. Why was he doing this? My heart wasn't ready to hear this. I loved Griff and I thought I was whole, but my heart was definitely still damaged from Creed. He was hurting me with every word. I turned away from him and wiped more tears that silently fell.

We pulled into my driveway and I was tempted to jump out of the car and run before the car came to a complete stop. I would likely end up breaking a leg, putting me back in the car with Creed as he took me to the hospital. When the car did come to a stop, I didn't jerk open my door and run either. I calmed myself before opening the door and getting out.

I didn't look back at Creed as I walked to my back door, and when I finally reached it, I knew he wasn't following me. I glanced over my shoulder then to see where he was and I saw his back as he walked across the yard toward his house. I should go inside. Let this night end and hopefully the emotions his words had stirred would end too.

"He saved me," I called out into the darkness. "I was a broken mess and Griff saved me," I added, wishing I would shut up, but my mouth was taking over. Creed turned then and looked at me. I couldn't see his face in the darkness but I knew he could see me from the porch light. "I loved you. I loved you so much it destroyed me. Losing you shut me down, my life no longer felt worth living. The darkness that surrounded me after what you did to me was so bad I didn't recognize myself anymore. I found her too. I was there too! I loved her too." I stopped then and choked back a sob. I was stronger now. I needed to say this. He needed to hear it. "Griff helped me heal." I added loud enough for him to hear me. Griff had been there when no one else had and his light had been what gave me life again. I didn't stand there and look out into the darkness toward him any longer. I'd said enough.

eighteen

NOVEMBER 13, 2019

My eyes flew open and for a moment I wasn't sure what had woken me. It was still dark in my room. Then I heard the knocking. Sitting up in bed, I rubbed my eyes and waited to make sure I wasn't still dreaming when the knocking came again. Tossing back the covers, I shivered and grabbed my throw to wrap around me then slipped on my faux fur-lined shoes before heading downstairs.

More knocking came and I realized it was my back door. I glanced at the time on the microwave before I turned to go into the living room. It was 2:36 AM. The knocking started again and I went to the door, not sure I should open it without being able to see who was out there. I stopped at the closed locked door.

"Who is it?" I asked.

"Me," Creed replied.

In that moment, I had a choice. Open the door or tell him to go home. Creed was my friend but tonight we'd both said things I wasn't sure I wanted to face yet. I still needed sleep and time to think about what he'd said and what I'd admitted to him.

"Sailor, please," he pleaded and I didn't weigh my options any longer. I might regret it, but I wasn't going to be able to send him away.

My hand closed over the cold brass knob and I took a deep breath before turning it. We hadn't finished our conversation tonight and he wanted to now. I had been sleeping but I hadn't gone to sleep easily. I'd tossed and turned for over an hour before exhaustion finally won out. Maybe he needed to say something so he could get some sleep.

I unlatched the screen door as my eyes locked on Creed. His hair was tousled as if he'd ran his hands through it several times and he was still wearing the clothes he'd had on earlier. A pair of faded jeans and a navy sweater. He stood there a moment in the freezing temperature and I pulled my throw tighter around me as I stepped back for him to enter.

Creed looked at me then at the door, as if he wasn't sure he was going to come inside. I was about to tell him to make up his mind because it was too cold for this when he moved to walk into the house. I quickly closed the screen and then the door behind him but didn't turn around to face him. I needed a moment to prepare to deal with whatever he needed to say. Perhaps if we had been able to talk six years ago, instead of him shutting me out, I wouldn't be so wounded still today.

His hand touched mine and I shivered but I wasn't sure if it was from his nearness or the fact his hand was still cold from being outside. I stayed still, not turning to look at him, and he laced his fingers through mine. I inhaled sharply. It was just our hands but it felt like much more. The air around us seemed to heat and I was struggling to breathe properly.

He tugged me to him and my back pressed against his chest. My breaths were becoming fast and shallow. I needed to pull myself away from him but I didn't. We stood there in the darkness of the living room. I waited for him to say something or for me to get the will to walk away and put some distance between us.

Neither of those things happened and when I felt the warmth of his breath on the curve of my neck, just before his lips touched my skin, I didn't care anymore about words. We'd said too much already. There were no words that could fix the past.

Creed's other hand ran down my arm and I felt the grip on my throw loosen as it slid down my body. I didn't feel the chill anymore. I felt warm, almost too warm. Creed's hand touched my waist and he gently turned me to face him.

His right hand slid into my tangled hair and he tugged at it enough to tilt my head back. Our gazes locked, just before his mouth covered mine. It wasn't painful but he wasn't exactly gentle either. The hard press of his lips felt as if he was placing a claim on me that we both knew he didn't have the right to do. My brain knew I should stop this but my body was clawing to get as close to him as possible.

With both of his hands now on my hips, he pushed me until my back was against the closed door. The possessive move made me slightly crazy. My hands slid into his hair and when his right hand eased down my bare thigh past the oversized flannel shirt I was wearing, I was ready to climb all over him. Right and wrong didn't matter to me in this moment.

Creed clasped his hand over my knee and pulled it up to his waist. The vulnerability I suddenly felt caused me to tense for only a moment. The hardness behind the zipper of his jeans made everything else fade beneath the desire flooding me.

My body took over and nothing else mattered but the pleasure. Grabbing his biceps, I raised my knee higher and rubbed against the temptation.

"Sailor," he groaned and his hand grabbed my other thigh, pulling it up so that my feet were no longer on the floor. I was pressed against the door, open to him. His mouth pulled back from mine and our eyes locked as he cupped my butt and rocked against me.

"Ah!" I cried out from the delicious pressure.

Creed's eyes heated as he moved a hand down until it slipped between my legs. I was lost the moment his fingers moved under my panties and began to stoke the tenderness. "Oh god," I moaned, clinging to him, afraid I would explode.

"I've dreamed about you," he told me in a husky whisper before his mouth began trailing kisses along my jawline while his fingers continued to explore.

If he wanted a response, he wasn't getting one. Words were becoming too difficult.

"So damn sweet," he said against my ear and I shivered, squeezing his arms until my nails dug into the skin. "I need you, Sailor."

He had me. I lifted my hips, forcing his finger inside me. "Yes!" I cried out at the entry.

"Fuck," he growled and then I was moving. He held me against him and walked the few steps to the sofa before laying me down. The burning hunger in his gaze made me tremble with excitement. I watched as he pulled his shirt over his head, dropped it to the floor and then went to his jeans. I'd known he would be beautiful naked, but the chiseled perfection seemed ridiculously unfair. I wanted to sit up and touch him. Run my fingers over him like I would a sculpture that enraptured me.

His hands moved to my shirt and with ease, he had it unbuttoned. When his hands went to my panties, he slowed and his gaze lifted to mine then went back to the white satin before he began easing them down my legs. What came next I wasn't expecting and the second he shoved my thighs open and lowered his head I stopped breathing.

Creed's tongue began to circle my clit then lick slowly between my folds. My hands gripped his hair and sounds came from me I didn't recognize. Nothing mattered. If I died that would be okay. Just so he didn't stop. Nothing had ever felt this amazing. He made a low sound in his chest and the vibration felt incredible. "Oh God!" I screamed and pulled at his hair.

With his tongue flat, he slowly licked until my orgasm burst free, causing me to shout his name among other things. By the time it eased, Creed had moved over me and the moment I opened my eyes to look at him, he slid inside of me. Another cry escaped me and I lifted my hips to meet his thrust.

"It's always been you," he whispered the words.

He began to rock his hips as each press into me became more forceful. I moved my right knee higher, wrapping my leg around his back and the position caused him to grow more intense. He pressed a kiss to my shoulder then a sharp bite from his teeth startled me. The pain shouldn't make my body ignite more, but it did. When he licked the spot he'd bitten, I felt my second orgasm beginning to build. I wanted him to bite me again. What was wrong with me?

"Harder," I begged him, thinking in that moment he couldn't do it hard enough. I wanted the pain with the pleasure.

He thrusted deeper and I screamed out. He bent his head again and licked at the bite then whispered in my ear, "You feel like heaven."

I dug my nails deeper into his arms and whimpered.

"Oh God, Creed!" I moaned, his words sending shocks of pleasure through my body. "Please," I begged, but I wasn't sure what I was begging for. Relief, more, I didn't know. I lifted my hips, making each entry harder and faster.

He stopped talking then and I stopped thinking. The coming rapture that was about to overtake my body made every cell tingle. I began to whimper and I felt it, knowing it was going to be stronger than the others.

Just when the explosion came over me, I heard Creed shout my name and his body jerk. Forcing my eyes open, I saw his head thrown back and the veins in his neck were visible as he reached his climax, my own body shaking as I moaned beneath him.

As my breathing slowed and I could inhale properly again, Creed moved to the side of me and pulled me into his arms. With his free hand, he grabbed the blanket on the floor beside us and covered our intertwined bodies with it. I wanted to say something, but I didn't know what. Sleep came quickly this time.

nineteen

I woke to a warm heavy body moving over me. Squinting, I could see it was morning and that Creed was pulling on his jeans. I didn't say anything as I watched him. Was he leaving? Should I ask?

When he started to turn toward me, I closed my eyes. I wasn't ready to be awake and deal with last night just yet. He was moving around again and I chanced a peek to see if he was continuing to get dressed. He was shirtless, putting a log in the fireplace.

I watched him build a fire and admired the way the muscles on his back moved with the task. I had been so busy watching his chiseled body, I missed the fact he was finished and now turning around. His eyes locked with mine and he gave me a crooked grin.

"Morning," he said.

I pulled the cover tighter against my naked body and returned his smile. "Good morning."

He ran a hand through his hair and it shouldn't look so good when he did that. I was mesmerized and if we were going to talk, he had to put his shirt back on. I couldn't concentrate if he had it off. I noticed claw marks on his upper arms and I gasped.

"I am so sorry," I said, my eyes flying to his face.

He frowned. "For what?"

I lifted my hand and pointed at his arm then grimaced.

He glanced down at it and then chuckled. When he looked back at me, he raised his eyebrows and nodded at my shoulder. "Don't apologize. I bit you."

Oh yeah…he had. Sitting up quickly, I tried to look at it but realized I couldn't see it. Then I realized I was topless and the covers were no longer covering that up. I grabbed for them and pulled them back up, before seeing if Creed caught that.

Creed smirked at me.

He'd seen all of me last night. It wasn't like I was hiding something from him. I scowled at him or did my best to scowl at him. It was hard to scowl at a beautiful man shirtless. I wanted to get up and go lick his chest, and then I wanted him to make me orgasm some more because I had never experienced anything like it.

Not even with Griff.

Griff.

I felt sick to my stomach. I was lusting over Creed and wanting to have sex with him again, not even considering Griff. My sweet, kind savior who loves me. I'd betrayed him. Last night I should have stopped things because of Griff. But I'd been too damn crazed to have Creed inside me to think of anything else.

I was a slut.

No. I was worse than a slut. I was a cheating slut!

I heard Creed sigh and I didn't look at him. I wrapped the covers around me tighter and stood up. I needed to get clothes on and I needed…I needed…we needed to talk. We should have talked last night. But no, we had gone at it like rabbits.

"Let me make some coffee and get the stove burning then we can talk," Creed said, as if he could read my mind.

I managed to nod my head.

"Sailor," Creed said, as he closed the distance between us.

I slowly raised my eyes from the floor to meet his.

He reached out and cupped my face with his hand. "Stop thinking whatever you're thinking. Go get clothes on because if you don't I'm going to bend you over the sofa and fuck you so that I can see your sexy ass bounce."

I gasped and my face heated then the space between my legs tingled. Oh, god I was a horny cheating slut.

"When you're clothed, we will talk," he said then bent down and kissed the tip of my nose. "Please go get clothes on. I'm only so strong."

I don't know if I was more worried about him doing what he threatened or the fact I was excited about what he had threatened to do that sent me hurrying up the stairs.

Once I was safely in my room, I went to the bathroom to do my morning routine then headed to my closet for leggings with the warm lining and a sweatshirt. Feeling safely dressed and trying hard not to think about being bent over the sofa by Creed, I took several deep steadying breaths.

Creed was in the kitchen when I returned, and I refused to even look in the living room. The damn sofa was in there. The place of my treachery.

I walked into the kitchen and Creed handed me a cup of coffee. I muttered a thank you, unable to make eye contact with images of him bending me over the sofa still fresh in my head.

"I'm not going to say I'm sorry. Nothing about last night do I regret," he said, walking over to sit down at the table, leaving me the spot closest to the fire.

I took a drink of my coffee and paused realizing it was exactly the way I drank it. I looked up at him then and he shrugged. "I told you I know you. I pay attention to you. I always have."

Not always. I caught myself from blurting that out. There had to be a better way to talk about this other than me shouting all the wrongs he'd done to me. He had shut me out after Cora's death. I just didn't know how to say it. How did I bring up the worst day of our lives?

I sat down and put my cup on the table. I wasn't ready for that conversation. It needed to happen, but right now, there was Griff.

"I'm a cheater," I said simply. That was the biggest issue I was dealing with currently.

He didn't respond right away. I wasn't sure he was going to. What was he supposed to say anyway "yeah you are" or "shit happens"?

"I love him," I added for my benefit because I did. I needed reminding.

"He was there for you when you needed someone. Of course, you love him. But are you in love with him?"

I opened my mouth to say "YES" but it didn't come out. Was I in love with him? Could I have so willingly had wild hot sex with another man if I was in love with him? Or was I just lonely and Creed was here to fill the need. I looked at Creed and the emotion in my chest that always came with him was there. It was more than needing sex. Could I love two men at once?

"You'll tell him. You won't be able to live with yourself if you don't. Just be sure what you want from him when you do."

What did that mean? "I want him not to hate me," I said, already knowing what I wanted.

He nodded once. "And that's your answer."

Frowning, I slammed my fist on the table a little too dramatically. "What is my answer? You're just confusing me."

"You want him not to hate you. If you were in love, you would want him to forgive you."

"Of course I want him to forgive me! That's what I meant," I shot back frustrated.

Creed raised an eyebrow. "Is it?"

"Stop," I said forcefully, standing up and walking away from the table. I needed space because I was close to hitting him.

I heard the legs of his chair scrap across the floor and his footsteps as he walked toward me. I stood at the kitchen sink staring straight out the window. I didn't want to believe that I wasn't in love with Griff. I hated the idea.

Creed's hands rested on either side of the sink caging me in. His chest was against my back and he was warm. My body wanted to melt against him, but my brain was currently calling the shots.

"I didn't want to want you. When I saw you in that apartment, I didn't want to feel anything. It was easier to forget the past because with it was the memory of Cora," he said her name with obvious pain. "But seeing you again only proved what I already knew. I could run from you, but you owned me and there was not a fucking thing I could do to make that go away."

I closed my eyes and wished his words didn't affect me. Right now, I was supposed to be thinking of my feelings for Griff. How to tell him and not lose him.

Creed ran the back of his hand down my arm then slid his arm around the front of my thigh until his fingers brushed the spot just between my legs. "I will never get enough of you, Sailor. Ever."

He began rubbing me then just hard enough for me to tremble with need. His erection pressed against my lower back and I let my head fall back on his chest. Creed slid his other hand under my sweatshirt until he was cupping my bare breast. I made a sound and I felt his breathing grow heavier. "I was wrong," he said in a thick voice. "Clothes didn't help. I need to fuck you now."

My leggings were pulled down with a hard tug and my panties went with them.

"Put your hands on the sink." It sounded like a command and that only ignited my hunger for him.

I heard his jeans unzip then his hands grabbed my waist. "Spread your legs and stick that ass out."

I did as told and he slammed into me so hard my knees gave way, but I held onto the sink for support.

"You make me crazy, Sailor," he said as he pumped into me. "I already fucking love you. I didn't need to see your tits jiggling braless under your shirt or have you bent over in front of me so your perfect ass was displayed. All I could think about was getting inside you." He was panting as he spoke. His breathing as ragged as mine.

His hand landed hard on my left butt cheek and I cried out.

"That's for making me want you so bad," he said, then began to caress the spot he had slapped. Much like he had licked where he bit me last night.

Being spanked was more exciting that I had imagined, and I wiggled in hopes he'd do it again. He did and this time, he squeezed the spot he slapped. "Keep that up and I'm going to bury my face in that ass."

That was not a threat, but I think he knew that. My orgasm began to build, and I wanted it. I wanted it so badly that nothing else mattered. Creed was inside me, giving me immense pleasure. He was all I cared about, or was I all I cared about? Was I completely selfish? Yes, I was.

His hand slid down and began to play with my clit as he pressed harder into me. "I love this pussy," he said in my ear then bit the lobe.

The sharp bite to the soft flesh combined with his finger rubbing me sent me over the edge of the cliff. I screamed his name and gripped the sink hard.

"FUCK!" Creed shouted, and his body went rigid behind me.

I felt another tremor race through me and my knees almost completely gave out when his arm wrapped around my waist and he pulled me against him. We stood there like that as our breathing returned to normal.

About Tomorrow...

I stared outside and accepted the fact I wasn't going to be able to stop this. Creed Sullivan was worse than any drug. Twice and I was addicted.

twenty

NOVEMBER 14, 2019

Griff hadn't responded to my text or the two voice messages I had left him. I needed to see him. We had to talk, and it wasn't a conversation that should be done on the phone. However, he was making it difficult to see him. I stared down at my phone in frustration then sent one more text telling him I wanted to come see him this weekend. Maybe then he'd get back to me.

I put the phone on the small table by the tub and laid my head back to relax. I'd decided a hot bubble bath would warm me up better than a fire when I got home from work. It was doing the trick, but the fact was I would have a cold house when I got out of the tub. I shivered thinking about it.

Creed had soaped me up in the shower this morning then thoroughly screwed me before leaving for work. He'd texted me twice today to tell me he missed me. I felt the smile on my lips as I thought about just how good this morning had been. If my body wasn't so obsessed with the way Creed made it feel, this would be harder. The looming fact that this was going to hurt Griff was clouding everything. Well, not in the moment I was screaming Creed's name but when I wasn't being sexually satisfied.

I was accepting the fact I was in love with two men. Loving Griff hadn't made me stop loving Creed. It had made it easier to live without Creed.

I heard the door downstairs open and close. I waited listening for steps on the stairs and then watched the doorway for Creed. He filled the entryway and his arms were full of wood.

"I'll get a fire going in your room," he told me then let his gaze fall to my naked breasts just above the water. "Let me dry you off," he added, then turned to go light the fire.

How did he do that? One look and my vagina was tingling. I would get frustrated with myself if it weren't for the fact I knew how good he was about to make me feel. I touched the area between my legs and winced at how tender it was. This morning in the shower had been the most intense hard sex we have had so far.

Creed walked into the bathroom again and picked up a towel. "Come here," he said.

When he was like this, I always obeyed. I couldn't stop myself. Standing up, I let the bubbles and water slide down my body while he watched before stepping out.

"You're about to get fucked wet," he threatened.

Smiling, I held up my hands and he wrapped the towel around me. "How was your day?" he asked as he pulled me against him.

"Great. I had three visitors that asked questions about the exhibit. Then I got to peek at the new stuff that arrived."

He held me in his arms keeping me warm. "Are you sore?" he asked me, sliding a hand between my legs.

I winced when he touched me and he grinned. "I'll kiss it and make it better," he told me and immediately went down on his knees in front of me. "Open."

I stared down at him, my mouth slightly open in a mix of awe and anticipation. His eyes lifted to meet mine then he pressed a kiss to my inner thigh, before placing his hands on both my thighs and leaning in to begin teasing me with such erotic pleasure I struggled to keep standing.

Sometime after eleven, the text alert on my phone woke me up and I opened my eyes. I was naked and pressed up against Creed's naked body with his arm around me. Trying not to wake him, I reached for my phone already knowing who it was. Guilt and dread filled me as I read the text from Griff.

"Sorry long two days. Turned in my paper and aced an important exam. Not sure if you coming this weekend is a good idea. I will be swamped with memorizing shit for Gross Anatomy. Let's plan for the middle of the week next week. Either I will come there or you come here. I will make it work. Love you. Talk soon."

I didn't feel sad this time. Normally when he put me off or said he couldn't come, I was sad. That emotion was gone. Sleeping with Creed wasn't justified and I knew that, but it was time to end it with Griff. He was never getting here and he was never going to let me come there. It would be Christmas before we saw each other.

This wasn't fair to Griff. I had only been in New England for three weeks and maybe if I'd given Griff more time, he would have figured a way to come see me. But if I was being honest with myself, Griff had been too busy for me since his classes had started. When I was in Nashville, he had called more at first but with each week he got deeper into this semester, I heard less from him. If we were meant to be, wouldn't he miss me as much as I had missed him?

I put my phone back and turned to look at Creed. His lashes fanned his cheekbones and his lips reminded me of all the wonderful things they could do. I wanted to kiss them until he woke up and rolled me on my back and entered me again. I didn't though. He needed sleep. Snuggling back into the bed, I closed my eyes and tried not to think about anything more than the man holding me.

NOVEMBER 15, 2019

When I woke the next morning, I was alone but a fire was blazing in the bedroom fireplace. I glanced at the time on my phone and it was after eight. Creed had a meeting at eight this morning in town on decisions about the lighthouse. The fire was going to need me to poke it soon, so I stretched and got out of bed to go tend to it and head downstairs to check on the other fires.

Stopping at the fireplace, my eyes went to the pictures I'd put there. The one with me and Griff smiling on our ski trip to Colorado last winter stared at me. I walked over and took it down. I couldn't deal with seeing this right now. Taking the photo, I walked over to the shelves where I had another picture of Griff and I in our cap and gowns. I picked it up too and placed both in the hallway closet. Turning, I headed to the kitchen.

Once I had coffee I sat down in the living room chair and read the text from Griff again. If I waited until I saw him in person, we may not be broken up for a month. He kept promising he'd come see me or I could come see him but that had yet to happen. His promises had little weight these days.

It was time I did this, dealt with the pain it was going to cause, and moved on. I couldn't see how Griff would be able to forgive me. At first that was my only concern. Keeping Griff and the relationship we had wasn't my desire anymore. I did love Griff. He had helped me heal in a way he would never understand, but since he moved to Boston, we hadn't been the same.

I was holding onto how we once were, not how we were now. I wanted to be important to him and if he hadn't changed so much then maybe we would still be that strong. Medical school was the most important thing in his life and I respected that. I just couldn't continue the growing apart. Every day that went by and he had less time for us…for me, I felt more disconnected. The man that had loved me so much was different. He had a life I wasn't a part of and this was only the semester of his first year in med school. I didn't see how we could survive this. It didn't excuse what I did. Forgiving myself wasn't going to come easy or soon, but I couldn't keep holding onto a man who I didn't love enough.

Truth was I had always wanted Creed, but I'd forgotten just how strongly I felt about him until he was back in my life. No matter what pain it caused Griff, I couldn't let Creed go. I was in love with him and being with him again had shown me that he was right. I loved Griff, but I wasn't in love with Griff. That place in my heart had been owned by Creed since I was too young to be sure when it happened.

I would text Griff one more time about the importance of him calling me. If I couldn't have this conversation with him in person then I was at least going to do it on a call and not a text message.

"Please, Griff, I need to talk to you today. Call me as soon as you have a moment."

Griff was busy, but he would make time for me if it sounded urgent. At least he once would…these days, I was never sure.

twenty-one

Clarks' parking lot was packed for a freezing November night. Smoke was rising from the chimney as we made our way to the front door. Creed let go of my hand to open the door and wave me inside. We were greeted by Lulu, and like the last time, she ate Creed up with her eyes. Unlike last time, I felt the need to glare at her in warning.

"Hiya, Creed. Want your regular table?" she asked in a sing-song voice I assumed she thought was cute. It wasn't.

He placed his hand on my lower back and leaned into me. "You want near the fire?" he asked me then kissed my temple. My annoyance at Lulu's flirting vanished. In its place was the warm rush from Creed's open display of affection.

"Yes, please," I said, smiling up at him.

He glanced at the hostess. "Close to the fire," he told her.

Lulu's flirty grin was gone as she turned to head in that direction. We followed her and I was doing my best not to smile brightly. I loved being with Creed, but in the back of my head was still the fact Griff hadn't called me back and I needed to tell him the truth. Not just about my being with Creed but about my past with Creed. I'd been in counseling when Griff and I met and he always assumed it was because of my mother. He needed to know the truth.

"Creed Sullivan and Sailor Copeland on a Friday night again." Fleur's voice carried over the music.

I stopped and turned to look at her, instead of sliding into the booth Lulu had brought us to. She was still very pregnant and appearing glamorous despite it. I hoped I pulled off pregnancy the way she did one day. The idea of me being pregnant unleashed a myriad of images in my head. I always wanted to be a mother and a wife, but those desires came after my time with Creed. Thinking of them now with Creed beside me made me ache for things I didn't deserve but desperately wanted.

Creed's hand was still on my back, and Fleur's gaze took that in as her smile grew into a knowing one. "Well, well, that didn't take long at all," she added and winked at me.

"Fleur," Creed said with a nod.

"You still have the magic it would seem," she said and shook her head as she grinned. "But then you two were bound to be together. Always were."

I wasn't sure how to respond to that and the assumption we were together. We were together, but I was also not broken up with my boyfriend. Creed and I hadn't sat down and discussed what it was we were doing either. Other than the obvious, which was having amazing sex and sleeping in the same bed.

"Jessie," Fleur called out to a male server at the table nearest to ours. "Get these two whatever they want. They're my friends," she added with emphasis. Then she turned back to us. "I'll be back to chat soon. Right now, we have a new line cook in the kitchen and Josh is about to kill him if he messes up again. I need to go run interference."

Creed waited for me to move into the booth then slid in beside me. We were facing the fire and the other tables were to our back, which gave a small amount of privacy. His hand rested on my thigh and I tried very hard not to think sexual thoughts. Jesse was about our age and he had impressive curly hair for a guy. He took our orders and left.

"Did you talk to Griff today?" he asked me for the first time since he'd come home from work. I had expected this question sooner.

I shook my head no. "I tried."

He squeezed my thigh. "He'll call."

Yeah but when? Next week?

"Damn if you two don't look cozy." We both looked up to see Derek Young standing beside our table with a smirk on his face.

"Evening, Derek," Creed said grinning at his friend.

Derek slid into the booth across from us and leaned forward on his elbows. "It took less than a week?" he asked still grinning.

Creed's hand squeezed my thigh again. "No, it took longer than a week. I've been working on getting her attention for a while."

I looked up at Creed frowning because that was not true. He winked at me then pressed a kiss to my forehead.

"Okay I came to visit but try not to make out with her while I'm sitting here," Derek said too loudly.

I blushed and ducked my head.

"Sorry, Sailor. I'm just giving Creed a hard time. It's been awhile since I had something like this to tease him about. Typically, he comes around with females that we all know we won't see again and we are thankful for that."

I pressed my lips together to keep from laughing and Creed chuckled.

"Your house looks good," Derek told him. "Sure is nice driving by and seeing those two houses lit up again. Having them empty was depressing and having someone that wasn't a Sullivan in your house was just wrong."

"It's good to be back home," Creed told him. "I didn't know how much I missed it until I came back."

"What about you? How are you handling the cold?" Derek asked me.

I lifted my shoulders with a shrug. "Okay, I guess. It's an adjustment but I'm learning to appreciate a good fire and an electric blanket."

Derek laughed and started to say something when our drinks arrived.

"I'm here with a date and need to get back over there to her. She's proving to be the high maintenance variety and I'm not sure there will be another date," he told us in a whisper as he stood back up. "I'll see you both around."

I watched him go back to the table across the room and got a look at the blonde he was with. Her hair was in a perfect smooth low ponytail and she was wearing a red sweater. Other than that, it was all I could see.

"He always finds something wrong with the women he dates. He's been doing it since he got his heart broken by Britney."

The mention of his heart being broken reminded me of Griff and I felt sick to my stomach. It was easy to pretend that Griff wasn't an issue when I was with Creed. Being with him made everything else seem unimportant. The happiness that came with having Creed in my life was so overpowering it masked the ugly that I had to face.

Like the fact I was currently on a date with a man I was in love with, while my boyfriend sat in an apartment fifty-five miles from here studying. I was a monster. A very selfish monster.

"Where did your head just go?" Creed whispered, slipping his arm around my shoulders and pulling me closer to him. He was too good at reading my expressions. I had never had someone read me so clearly and it was unnerving at times.

I didn't have a chance to answer when a woman in her mid-thirties appeared at our table. "I'm sorry to interrupt, but are you Sailor Copeland? We're having an argument over at our table and I'm here visiting friends, but I live in Georgia and I've seen you on all the magazines. I know it's you. They think I'm crazy." She was standing there with her hand on her hip, looking convinced of who I was and ready to go gloat to her friends.

Before Creed could cover for me, I decided I had lied enough for one week. I wasn't about to add to it and honestly, I wasn't in the mood to let anyone down right now. I had enough of that coming. I nodded. "Yes, I am, but I like to keep a low profile. Would you mind keeping that info at your table?" I asked her as sweetly as I could.

Her eyes blazed with excitement. "I knew it! I won't tell a soul, honey. Don't you worry. I just knew it was you. You're even more beautiful in person. Just like your daddy."

"Thank you," I said, keeping the smile I didn't feel in place. I may have just made a mistake, but I didn't think people in this town or bar were going to come flocking to me because my dad was a country singer.

"Y'all carry on now. I'm sorry to interrupt," she said, then with one last bright smile, she turned and hurried away.

I could feel Creed's eyes on me. I lifted my gaze to meet his. "I just didn't want to disappoint her. She seemed so sure of herself and excited."

A small smile touched his lips then he lowered those lips and pressed them against mine. In that moment, nothing else mattered. Creed could make it all disappear so very easily.

twenty-two

NOVEMBER 16, 2019

The kitchen was bright from the morning sun, the house smelled of coffee and firewood, the colorful leaves had almost all fallen outside my window, and Creed was sitting on the sofa in the living room, waiting on me to join him. It was a late fall Saturday morning in New England, and it was perfect… except that I was standing in my warm cozy kitchen staring at the phone in my hand as it began to ring.

Griff was finally calling me.

"It's him," I called out to Creed. "I'm going to step outside," I added. Somehow telling Griff all of this in front of Creed seemed wrong. He at least deserved privacy.

I went to open the kitchen door when Creed walked into the room. "It's still below freezing this morning. I'll go to my house. Let me know when you're done," he said, before pressing a kiss to my cheek.

The moment the door closed behind him I answered the call.

"Hello," I said, my stomach was already in tangled knots.

"Hey, sorry I didn't call you yesterday. Your text seemed important but time got away from me."

I was used to this excuse by now. Time was always getting away from him. His world was med school and I was proud of him. He'd worked hard to get where he was and I understood his dedication. However, our relationship hadn't survived it.

"I understand," I replied, still not sure how to explain everything and feeling like a jerk for doing it on the phone, but if not now when? I didn't want to stop things with Creed until I ended them with Griff because I didn't know when that would happen. I had this call and I had to take it.

"What's up?" he asked, and I heard pages turning in the background. Was he studying?

Rip off the bandage. That's what I had to do. Get it done.

"Griff, when we met, I was a mess. I know you remember the counseling and my unwillingness to get close to you. You had to work hard to get me to go on that first date," I began. He said nothing so I continued.

"I never explained much about it and you assumed it was my mother and the life I'd lived with her that had sent me to counseling and made me so hard to get close to but it wasn't. Growing up I told you about my summers at Gran's, what I didn't tell you was the twins that lived next door. I was close to them. The girl and I became best friends as we grew up and the boy…well, I fell in love with him. He was my first. I didn't think I'd ever love anyone else. We had a history that was intense and when we found his sister dead from an overdose the summer I was seventeen, he never spoke to me again. I didn't know why. I'd lost my best friend and my boyfriend on the same day. I was damaged."

I paused then taking a deep breath.

"Okay, I'm glad you told me all this. Are you dealing with it now that you're there? The memories?" He asked.

"Not exactly. I began dealing with it the first day at your apartment," I said, then closed my eyes to get this over with.

This was where it was going to be hard. "Creed Sullivan was the boy and I hadn't seen him in six years until that day."

There was silence and I didn't know how to keep going.

"Okay, what is this about, Sailor? That you didn't tell me you knew Creed?"

Another deep breath. "I never stopped loving Creed. With you being there and us not seeing each other, I've had time here alone and Creed moved in next door to his family's house. We've…been together. I wanted to do this in person, but you never had time and I couldn't keep lying. I needed you to know."

He said nothing.

I didn't know what else to say.

We sat there in silence, the only sound the crackling of the fire in the living room. The sick knot in my stomach was still there, but there was also a relief that came with telling Griff.

"Are you breaking up with me?" he asked.

His question confused me. I didn't want to say the words but maybe he needed me to. I was going to let him break up with me. I was the one who cheated. I was the one who should be dumped.

"I have wonderful memories with you and you saved me when no one else could. I will always love you for that. But you have medical school and time for a relationship isn't possible." And I was in love with Creed, but I'd already told him that and I didn't want to rub it in his face.

"Goodbye, Sailor," he said then ended the call.

I sat there holding the phone and looking down at it as tears filled my eyes. It hadn't been dramatic, but then Griff wasn't a dramatic person. I had hurt him and I hated that. I didn't want to hurt him. He'd always been so good to me. He had loved me and brought me back to life. In the end, I had tossed that in his face and walked away via a phone call. I was a terrible person. Setting the phone down, I pulled my knees up to my chest and buried my face in them and cried.

Griff had been a part of my life I would always cherish. Losing him was hard and felt like a piece of me was dead. However, I knew that losing him was easier than losing Creed. I'd done that once and I wasn't willing to go through that again. I wanted Griff to find happiness and he deserved to be loved the way I had thought I had loved him.

He deserved to be loved the way I loved Creed.

I'm not sure how long I sat there like that when Creed walked back into the house. He said nothing sitting down beside me. Gently, he pulled me into his arms, and I went willingly. More tears came as I let him comfort me when I didn't deserve comfort. He pressed his mouth against the top of my head and I closed my eyes, letting him try and soothe me. I didn't think anything would make this better. Griff was such a good man and what I'd done was unforgivable.

Creed said nothing and I was thankful for that. I just needed his arms around me right now. Talking wasn't something I was ready for and I didn't think Creed was the one who should listen to my ramblings. There were some things I needed to keep to myself.

Creed covered me with a blanket then leaned back and moved me to lay against his chest again. We sat there in the silence while my tears eased and then dried up. I stared at the dwindling fire in front of us and wondered if I'd done the right thing. Should I have gone to Boston and forced Griff to find time to talk to me? Telling him over the phone had felt like my only option but now it added to my guilt.

I had never broken up with anyone in my life. Maybe this was normal to feel so terrible. Creed had been the one to desert me and he'd been the only other relationship I'd had. Was I being too hard on myself? The cheating was real. I'd definitely been wrong there, but I had been honest and broken things off. Did that ease my guilt any?

No. It didn't.

"I love you, Sailor Moon," Creed said, as he began stroking my hair.

And that was why I had been able to hurt Griff…I wanted nothing in the world more than I wanted Creed Elijah Sullivan's love.

twenty-three

NOVEMBER 17, 2019

Another Sunday night at home alone and now I was wishing I had gone with Creed. Dalm had called him Friday to ask if he could play with Kranx tonight at Red's. I couldn't bring myself to go with him. It was too close to Griff and his life in Boston. The last time I'd been there, the females had thrown themselves at Creed. I wasn't sure I could handle that just yet. I was too emotionally screwed up. Creed had understood or at least he had said he understood.

My quiet home was suddenly too quiet and too empty. I drank some coffee, hoping it would keep me awake until Creed got back. He had said he'd come here tonight, which was no different from every other night since we had reconnected and slept together. We hadn't talked about a relationship yet or how things were going to work.

He had been giving me time to deal with my ending a four-year relationship and I was thankful for that. Although, I knew we soon needed to discuss us and eventually talk about the past.

There was a lot of pain there that needed clearing. At least for me.

A knock on my door startled me and I jerked my gaze from the television I hadn't been watching to stare at the door. It was close to nine, which meant it had been pitch black outside for hours and I wouldn't be able to see who it was unless they moved left and stood in the porch light. Standing up, I walked over to the window to check if I could see and was unsuccessful.

I opened the wooden door and froze as I locked eyes with Griff. I didn't reach for the lock on the screen door. I didn't do anything. I was worried I might throw up. My stomach was not okay.

He had his hands stuffed in the front pocket of his black wool coat and a scarf I'd bought him when he moved to Boston wrapped around his neck. Neither of us said a word and I wondered if I was supposed to say something. I didn't know what to say if he was waiting on me. I'd said it all.

"Can I come in?" he asked me, and I knew it was freezing outside…literally. I'd just checked the weather. I nodded, figuring it was the least I could do. I'd cheated on him and broken up with him. Letting him freeze outside seemed like a bad idea.

Reaching for the latch on the screen, it felt like I was moving in slow motion. I unhooked it and then opened it up for him. He walked past me and into my Gran's house for the first time. If he had come that first weekend I was here, like we had planned, would we be in the place we are now? No, probably not, but we would still have problems. I just wouldn't have acted on my feelings for Creed, but they'd have been there all the same. They were there the first day I saw him again; I'd just thought I'd overcome the way I felt for Creed.

"It's exactly like you described it," he said, as he stood in the middle of the living room looking around.

I said nothing. I just closed the door and waited for him to say why he was here. He'd told me goodbye on the phone and it had sounded final. His being here made it feel less final and

I didn't know how to feel about it. Part of me wanted to text Creed immediately, so he'd know Griff was here. Not that he would come racing back but just so he would know.

The other part of me felt like I owed Griff my full attention and texting Creed was insensitive. I stood there and did nothing.

Griff sighed heavily then turned his attention to me. "I'm not just letting you go, Sailor. I love you. I planned my future around you…around us. You're my best friend. I can't just let you tell me it's over because some guy that hurt you in the past came back into your life. He hurt you before, so what's keeping him from doing it again? I would never just walk away. I'm here proving that to you."

Oh, god no. Please not this. I was not ready for this. I didn't think this would happen. My chest hurt, my stomach was sick, and I felt positive I was going to cry at any moment. How did I handle this? The truth. I had to remember to stick to the truth.

"The past with Creed, it was…complicated. We found his sister dead from a drug overdose. Neither of us knew what she had been going through because that summer, instead of paying attention to the change in Cora, we were parking and having sex any chance we could get. Finding Cora like that, it was hard. It destroyed both of us, but Creed was her twin. He didn't just walk away from me. He was dealing with losing his twin."

Griff nodded. "I know all about Cora. Chet explained what you left out once I could think enough to talk about our conversation. But Sailor, y'all were kids. Hell, I thought I loved Sarah Norris at seventeen years old. That doesn't mean anything." He took a step toward me and I stiffened so he stopped. "I've had time to process things and I know this is partly my fault. You came here to be near me and I haven't made seeing you a priority. You were lonely and I understand that. Then," he throws his hand out with a look of disgust, "moody musician from your past walks in and sees you are vulnerable and works a fucking angle."

"It wasn't like that," I argued, but he didn't hear me or care.

"I love you, Sailor. I won't let you make this choice and hurt us both."

Creed wasn't a mistake. Griff was giving me excuses and I didn't want excuses for what I'd done. I had made a choice and it was the one I wanted. Seeing Griff again and hearing him say he loved me made words difficult. He wasn't accepting the truth and I was struggling with the strength to force him to listen to it. The love I had for Griff was strong enough to make me want to protect him.

"Griff, I love you. That isn't enough though. I am *in love* with Creed. I think I always have been." I hated saying the words again and this time to his face, but he was forcing me to.

Griff scowled and shook his head. "Really? You think what you feel for him is different than what we have? A grownup relationship that didn't start when we were children. I would never, NEVER walk away from you the way he did. No matter what happened because I am a man. What we have is different and what you feel is different because it's the kind of thing adults feel. It's not that silly, goofy shit you feel as a kid. It's the hard times, the good times, the boring as hell times. It's what is real, Sailor."

I knew he believed everything he was saying, and in most cases, he was right. Just not in our case. Yes, some young loves didn't work, okay most didn't, but what Creed and I had…have was different. We were the few that found our soulmate at a young age.

"I don't want to hurt you anymore. Standing here arguing with you about this is not helping anything," I pleaded with him. I didn't want to tell him how very wrong he was and point out the reasons why. I'd done enough damage. Tears were stinging my eyes and I wished more than anything that this was over.

Griff closed the distance between us and I froze, unsure what to do. He wasn't listening to me and I was starting to feel guilty that he was here without Creed knowing. I should have texted Creed and told him. This felt like I was lying to Creed and now that Griff was in front of me and so close to me, I wanted to scream from the confusion of it all.

"Do you know where this man you think you are in love with is right now?" he asked me.

I nodded, hoping Griff wasn't wanting to go brawl it out with Creed and thankful Creed was an hour away from here.

"Are you sure?" he asked me then.

"Yes. He's at Red's. He has a gig tonight with that band," I told him, feeling as if he was now accusing Creed of something.

Griff snarled at the explanation. "Yeah, he's at fucking Red's. I was there an hour and a half ago. I needed to drink until I wasn't hurting so damn bad. Imagine my surprise when I walked in and saw the man who had taken the only woman I have ever loved away from me sitting in a corner with some bimbo on his lap. He was smiling and acting like he owned the damn world while he had just taken my world away from me."

My stomach churned and I felt bile rise in my throat. I was going to be sick. I didn't want to believe Griff, but I knew him enough to know he wasn't a liar. Griff was honest and straight forward. He didn't do cool or play games. He was practical and dependable. I knew from the look on his face that everything he was telling me was true.

The tragedy of it all was it changed nothing.

Creed had said he loved me, but he had never said we were exclusive. He had never promised me a future. He had promised me orgasms and he'd delivered. That was it. Knowing this didn't make it hurt less. My chest felt as if it had been ripped open and I knew as the tears streamed down my face I deserved this. Every moment of it.

"Okay, if that's what you needed to say, you said it," I managed to get out over the emotion clogging my throat. I moved to the door then and opened it. "You can go. We've said all there is to say."

Griff didn't move. "I didn't come here to hurt you. I came here to tell you that you're making a mistake and throwing us away for nothing. I forgive you, Sailor. I love you too much not to."

I shook my head and wiped at the stupid tears that had fallen. I wasn't going to cry in front of Griff. "I slept with another man while we were together. Maybe you can forgive that but I can't. I may have made a mistake with Creed, but it is done. I care about you enough to want you to have someone worthy of your love. You deserve to be loved completely. You deserve someone's whole heart. You can never have mine," I stopped there. It was that simple. Even if Creed and I weren't what I had thought. Even if he was damaged and could never love me alone. I could never love Griff the way he should be loved.

Griff ran his hand over his face and sighed. "When you come to your senses call me. I won't wait forever, Sailor but I will wait."

I said nothing but stood there looking at the floor and holding the door open. He paused as he was walking out and I thought he was going to say more. He didn't and I was thankful for that small gift. Once he was outside, I latched the screen and closed the door. Standing there for a moment, I considered what would happen next. Then I reached up and bolted the door.

Tonight, nothing would happen. I wasn't ready to face Creed. I didn't know what to say to him or how to say it. I just needed to sleep in my bed and be alone.

Images of Creed with another woman on his lap plagued me as I took the steps to get ready for bed. I started to take a shower and realized the last time I'd been in there had been with Creed. Instead I went to the guest bathroom and bathed. Tears fell silently as tonight replayed in my head and I wondered if this would be the moment that I never forgot. Would I regret this decision the rest of my life?

twenty-four

JULY 22, 2014
MILLER STATE PARK, NEW HAMPSHIRE

The night sky was so clear out here that we could see every star. Creed's hand held mine as we laid in the bed of his truck, taking in the beauty around surrounding us. When he had asked me if I wanted to go to Monadnock Mountain on our date tonight I'd thought it seemed like an odd choice, but now we were here, I realized it was perfect. This summer Gran had allowed me later nights out with Creed and sometimes Cora, but she was with her boyfriend more and more.

Next summer we would all be high school graduates and getting ready to go off to college. Thinking about it scared me because I wouldn't have our summers anymore. Creed and Cora kept talking about us hiking the Appalachian Trail next summer or at least the northern half of it. If Creed was going to be there then I was all for it. I wasn't a hiker like the two of them were though. Nashville wasn't filled with hiking trails like New Hampshire was.

I felt Creed's head turn and I knew he was looking at me now and not the sky. I met his gaze and smiled. He was the most beautiful boy I had ever seen. I could look at him all day and never get bored. I didn't tell him this though or he'd think I was insane. Sometimes I thought I might be when it came to him. Loving someone as much as I did Creed was new to me and frightening. I'd always stayed closed off and protected my emotions. I'd learned at an early age from my parents that if you loved, you could get hurt. They'd hurt me plenty until I had gotten old enough to keep my feelings for them locked down.

With Creed, I had gone all in and every moment I was with him, I was happy. He made me happier than I'd ever thought I could be. Leaving him after this summer and going back to Nashville pained me to think about. I didn't want to leave him ever.

While my head was full of all the fears, hopes, and wishes where Creed was involved, Creed reached over and touched my cheek then leaned in to press his lips to mine. Kissing him was my favorite thing in the world. I moved closer to him and pressed my hand on top of his and kissed him back. He always tasted of peppermint.

His hand slid down my neck, and I let my hand rest on is face while he pulled my leg up over his. I felt the sundress I was wearing slide up my thigh, but we had made out heavy many times and it didn't bother me. I loved getting as close to Creed as I could. I made a sound in my throat that encouraged him and his hand moved under my sundress until he was cupping my bottom. That was exciting and my breathing was coming quicker.

Creed stopped kissing me, but he didn't move his face away from mine.

"I love you, Sailor," he whispered.

"I love you, too," I replied, smiling at the sweetness of his words.

His hand slid between my upper thighs then and I felt his finger slip inside the satin of my panties. I stopped breathing all together as he began to explore me. My right hand squeezed his upper arm and I managed to suck in some oxygen, just before his finger entered me. "Oh god." My words sounded like a moan, and if it didn't feel so good, I would be embarrassed.

Creed began kissing me again, and I tried to keep up while he made me feel things I hadn't before. When I thought I couldn't take much more and the pressure building inside was going to explode, he pressed me onto my back and came with me covering my body with his.

I knew what he wanted to do and I wanted it just as much. I'd never done this before but only because Creed was the only one I wanted to lose my virginity to.

"If you're not ready, I can wait. I'll wait as long as you want me to," he told me in a deeper voice than normal.

We only had a little over a month left of our summer together. I didn't want to miss anything. "I'm ready," I told him.

He bent his head down and kissed my cheek then my jawline, before hovering above my lips. "I'll love you forever," he said softly.

And I believed him.

twenty-five

NOVEMBER 18, 2019

My alarm went off too soon and getting dressed had been a chore. My sleep had been fitful and dreams of Creed hadn't helped me. Once I was ready for work, I headed downstairs, shivering at the cold as I reached the bottom step and knowing I didn't have time to start a fire. I'd warm up in my car on the way to work.

I glanced at the coffee pot in the kitchen and decided I'd wait until work for that too. There were at least two Dunkin' Donuts on my way to the museum; I could stop at one of those if the lines weren't too long.

Grabbing my coat, I pulled it on and then wrapped a red scarf around my neck. I knew when I walked out the door, I was going to want to look over at Creed's. See if his Jeep was there or if he'd not come home. I had put my phone on silent last night and turned on the sound machine to drown out any calls or knocks from him. I was going to have to check my phone for missed calls and texts eventually, but I wasn't ready for that yet.

None of that mattered, though, when I opened the back door and found Creed sitting there with steam coming from the coffee cup in his hand. His dark hair looked like he'd just gotten out of bed, but the darkness under his eyes made me think he didn't sleep at all. The urge to comfort him and kiss his beautiful face pulled at me, but I kept my distance. Last night had been emotionally draining and I didn't have the energy for this confrontation. Not yet.

"Morning," he said as his cool, even gaze settled on me.

"Hello," I replied.

He took a drink of his coffee and studied me a moment. "I called you and texted you last night."

I glanced down, not wanting to look at him. "I haven't checked my phone notifications this morning."

He said nothing and we stood there in silence for far longer than was comfortable.

"What happened that I don't know about, Sailor?" he asked finally.

There was no putting this off, but I wasn't ready to talk about the girl in his lap last night. I didn't have the mental strength for that. I was too sleep deprived, and I needed to get to work without black mascara running own my face.

"Griff came here," I said.

Creed took another drink and waited. He wanted more information than that it would seem.

"He was upset. He said he could forgive me and that he loved me. He said a lot of things," I stopped then because the one thing he had said that had caused me to lock Creed out last night was the one thing I was not going to bring up right now. I needed more time to process it.

Creed nodded once then straightened from his relaxed lean he had been doing on the porch railing. "I see," he said simply.

He saw what? I started to ask when he began to walk away. He was just leaving. He had no more questions. Nothing.

"You're leaving?" I asked him.

He paused then turned back to look at me. His eyes were hooded from the morning sun and he was just far enough from me I couldn't make out his expression very well. "You have a decision to make, Sailor. I won't beg. I'm not Griff," he said then continued across my backyard toward his.

My heart hurt and yet I wanted to pick up something and hurl it at his head. I had told him about Griff coming here last night, but he hadn't mentioned the woman he'd gotten friendly with in the bar. He believed this was about me choosing between him and Griff. That decision had been made already and Griff was no longer an option. However, I wasn't sure Creed was either.

I loved him, but I didn't trust him.

Getting in my car, I cranked it up and had to wait a few minutes so the window defrosted enough that I could scrape the ice off. I didn't think about the fact Creed had handled this for me last week when it had happened. I wasn't one to rely on anyone. My mother had made sure I wasn't dependent on others by never being there when I had a problem.

The drive to work was quick, but I hadn't stopped for coffee. I'd be stuck with Albert's strong stuff that he brewed. I would need the caffeine to focus on the new exhibit's opening day to the public. It was a Monday and I wasn't sure how much foot traffic we would get.

Ambre greeted me when I walked inside the building. She was busy at the welcome desk straightening things that didn't need straightening. She was always moving and rearranging. I wondered if she could share some of her energy with me.

"It's the day," she said cheerfully. "I didn't sleep very much from all the excitement. I wondered if we should move the eighteenth century closer to the front, but Albert said I wasn't to touch it. What do you think?" she asked but didn't give me a chance to answer her. "Never mind I will figure it out. Albert is in the back opening crates that came in this weekend. Go make sure he isn't making a mess and see if he wants me to go pick up breakfast."

I simply nodded and headed back to the kitchen area where I knew Albert's coffee would be.

"I think I'll go pick up an array of pastries," Ambre called out. "Do you have a request?"

I shook my head. "No, thank you. I'm not hungry." I doubted I would be hungry anytime soon.

Finding the kitchen empty, I sighed in relief and pinched the top of my nose as I leaned back against the wall. Had my choosing Creed over Griff been a mistake? I still believed Griff deserved more. I'd cheated and going back to Griff, even though he was willing to forgive me, wasn't an option. However, I had planned my future with Griff and now it was gone.

Creed had come back into my life like a whirlwind reminding me how I felt about him, being there every time I needed someone, and then there was the life altering amazing sex. Had I let all that cloud my vision? I knew Griff wouldn't lie to me. There had been a female on Creed's lap last night.

Loving Creed wasn't enough.

I had to be able to trust him as much as I had trusted Griff. We weren't teenagers in love anymore. Griff was right. We were adults now and love was shown differently. Not with hot sex.

I hated this. All of it.

"The exhibit isn't in here," Albert said gruffly as he walked into the room and went to the coffee pot.

"Yeah," I agreed.

He poured a cup and then handed it to me. "Drink it black. You need it," he said to me then went and poured him a cup.

I stared down at the dark liquid not sure anyone other than Albert could drink this stuff black.

"Life sucks then it goes on," Albert said, and I lifted my gaze to him. He shrugged. "It is a fact, Sailor. You'll find happiness and shit while you travel the path of life but you keep on going."

I wasn't sure Albert had ever said that many words to me or to anyone at one time. "How do you keep from being the shit that happens?" I asked him.

He grinned then. "You're not the shit that happens. You're young and you will make mistakes that make you feel like shit. It makes you tough and gives you a resilience to survive when things truly go to hell."

I wasn't so sure I hadn't already experienced the worst in life but I nodded. "Thanks."

He took a drink of his coffee while studying the wall over my head. "It's best to learn to find your happiness now. Whatever it is. Find it and hold onto it. That's what helps get you through the shit."

I didn't have time to think of a response before he walked out of the room.

twenty-six

NOVEMBER 22, 2019

It was almost time to close the museum when the door opened again. Ambre had already left because she had a plane to catch. She was headed to Ohio to spend the next week with her daughter and grandkids for Thanksgiving. Albert was in the back still working. I was left with watching the front and locking up.

I walked back around the counter where I had been putting away the brochures to greet the visitor when my eyes locked on who had walked in. "Dad?" I said in shock then ran toward him as he opened his arms.

Throwing myself in his embrace, I fought back tears. This week had been a lonely one and Creed hadn't been home most nights. I looked for the lights in his house and rarely saw them on. Seeing a friendly face made my resolve to be tough crack.

"Hey, my Sailor girl," he said as he held me and kissed the top of my head. "Miss me?"

I nodded my head against his chest and held all my emotions in check, before leaning back and smiling up at him. "I can't believe you're here."

"You sent me the text about your new job and I wanted to come check it out and see you. I'll be in Germany next week for Thanksgiving."

I couldn't remember the last time my dad spent a Thanksgiving or Christmas with me. He was always traveling. Then there was the one year he spent Christmas in Australia with his new wife. They'd been divorced by the next year, but he had been in Los Angeles then.

"I'm not sure I will be going to Nashville for Thanksgiving. Mom hasn't called and said she was planning something. I doubt she's in town."

He frowned. "What about Griff's family? Don't they do Thanksgiving up big?"

Griff's family…I had spent Thanksgiving with them the past few years. It was the perfect big event with kids running around and weird drunk uncles and pumpkin pie. I had loved going to this family's holidays. I'd miss that.

"We, uh, broke up," I said, not wanting to give dad details.

"Really? I wasn't expecting that. I thought the boy was smarter than that."

"It was my decision," I told him, not wanting him to harbor any ill will toward Griff.

He squeezed my arm gently. "I am sure you had your reasons. Now, what about we go to my penthouse at the Four Seasons in Boston? I'll have dinner brought in. You can tell me about life here and stay the night. Tomorrow, I fly out early afternoon. We can do brunch before I go."

Not going home to an empty house and wondering where Creed was sounded perfect. I nodded. "Sounds great. Let me get my coat and purse," I told him. I wasn't sure when I'd see my dad again or get to spend time with him. This would be the distraction I needed to get through the weekend.

I hurried and got my things then let Albert know I was leaving and that I'd lock up on my way out. Glancing down at my phone to see if I had any missed messages, I pushed the disappointment aside when I didn't. My dad was here, and I wasn't going to let Creed fill my thoughts.

When I stepped outside, a black limo was directly in the front. Dad was already inside and the driver was opening the door for me to follow. I slid in and sat my purse down.

"Here you go," Dad said, holding out a glass of red wine to me. "You look like you need it. When was the last time you got a good night's rest?"

I should have figured he wasn't fooled by my acting. I had never been good at it. Even Albert had been able to tell I was struggling this week. He'd made several comments about life in his odd way. I took a drink of the wine and sighed leaning back on the cream leather seat.

"Thanks. I do need one or five," I told him. "This has been a busy week. The new exhibit at the museum--"

"Is not what has kept you awake at night," Dad interrupted me. "What happened with Griff?"

I hadn't talked about this with anyone. Griff had been my best and only friend. Having my dad to talk to was better than having no one. I didn't have a tight relationship with my dad, simply because we didn't see much of each other. We never had. However, when I was around him, I still felt like the little girl who had once so desperately wanted his attention.

"I wasn't in love with him. I love him, but it wasn't enough," I said, hoping that was all Dad pushed me to admit.

Dad took a drink of the whiskey in his glass. "You figure that out on your own or did another guy help you with that knowledge?"

I cut my eyes at my father and he chuckled. "What honey? I'm a man. I write songs about relationships. I know more about this shit than you give me credit for."

I closed my eyes and rested my head on the back of the seat. "Creed Sullivan. He was Gran's neighbor all those summers I came to Portsmouth. He had a twin, Cora, and the three of us spent every day together. Then we got older, things changed, I fell in love with Creed, we had some perfect times together," I paused to take in a deep breath. "Then one day we found Cora dead from a drug overdose. She'd been battling depression and no one knew. She was always so full of life, but the year before, her volleyball coach had raped her. She hadn't been able to tell anyone. So, she left it in a letter beside her bed then took several bottles of medication from her mother's bathroom and went to an abandoned barn two streets over." I stopped again hating the memory and the image of Cora. She'd known we would find her. It had been our place to go…to be alone.

"Creed and I found her that day. He never spoke to me again. He shut me out. After her funeral, I didn't see him until the day I moved back here."

Dad let out a low long whistle. "Damn, honey. That's tough." He took another drink of his whiskey. I heard him swallow, even if my eyes were still closed. "So, you saw Creed again and realized you weren't done loving him? Is that what I am getting from this?"

I nodded my head then lifted it and opened my eyes to look at my father. "It wasn't fair to Griff," I said.

He studied the drink in his glass a moment then looked back at me. "Are you losing sleep because you miss Griff?"

"No," I replied. "Creed and I…we aren't talking right now. I thought he loved me. He said he did. I'm just not sure if I can trust him. The truth is I'm afraid I love the boy he was and I don't know the man he has become. I'm so mixed up and confused."

Dad nodded. "But you don't regret breaking things off with Griff?" he asked.

I shook my head. "No, I just hate that I hurt him."

Dad reached over and covered my hand with his. "Ignoring things doesn't make them go away. If you avoid the confrontation, you lose the relationship. Trust me I know. I've lost several wives that way. You gotta go talk to Creed. Tell him the truth. Tell him how you feel. Face it. Because you may just lose him again and there won't be a third chance."

I sat there thinking that over. Was I avoiding him or was he avoiding me? Did it matter who was doing the avoiding? I didn't want to lose Creed. I felt complete when I was with him. I wanted to understand where we stood and if we had a future. I could let him break my heart now or prolong it. I was tired of wasted time with Creed.

It may be that for once my dad was right when it came to relationships.

twenty-seven

NOVEMBER 23, 2019

When I pulled my car into the driveway, I looked over at Creed's house, but his Jeep wasn't there. I'd spent the entire limo ride back from Boston to my car in Portsmouth alone, thinking about what I was going to say to him. I was prepared and anxious, but it seemed I'd have to wait longer.

Walking inside the dark, cold house didn't help my mood. In less than a week, Creed had made his mark here. I had memories here with him that made me blush and made my heart hurt. Dad had asked me last night that if I had known Creed wasn't ready for an exclusive relationship would I still have cheated on Griff.

My answer had been yes. I felt guilty about that but what was done was done. I should have broken things off with Griff before cheating; I messed up. I didn't regret breaking up with Griff, but I did miss him.

I went to take a shower after starting the fire in the living room. Once I was refreshed and dressed in leggings and a hoodie, I decided to go for a walk. It was sunny and forty-five degrees. Granted in Nashville that would be considered cold, but I was starting to enjoy the weather when it got above forty degrees. I put on a coat and gloves, though, before heading back outside. Being outside kept me from getting in a funk while I waited for Creed to come home. I considered calling him but chose not to. I could wait.

I didn't get very far down the road when Jack's truck slowed beside me. "How's the firewood?" he asked with his window down.

I shaded my eyes from the sun with my hand and looked up at him. "Great, thank you," not sure if firewood could be bad.

He chuckled. "I mean do you have enough? I know you burn fires for heat in that house daily. Wasn't sure if you wanted me to go ahead and get you some more before it's gone."

Oh. I hadn't thought about that. "I'm not sure," I replied honestly. "I don't know how to gauge that."

Jack gave me a wide grin. "I can stop by and check."

"Thank you," I told him. "If I need more, just tell me how much. I'll get you the money."

He winked. "I know you're good for it. Enjoy the sunshine," he said then rolled up his window and drove away.

I started walking again when I paused to glance back toward the house to see if Jack was stopping now to check. I didn't see Jack, but I did see Creed's Jeep pulling into his drive. I watched him until he disappeared behind the house. I had been so ready to go face him when I got home, but now I was nervous. Unsure if he'd want to talk to me.

Standing there looking back down the road, I battled with myself over going to him now. My dad's warning about avoiding confrontation had me walking toward Creed's house. I didn't want to be my dad. I loved him, but he had left a lot of pain in his wake.

It wasn't Creed I saw when I came around the corner of his house but a female. One I recognized from the apartment in

Boston, Ember. I stood there staring at her as she laughed at something as she walked toward the back of the house, carrying a Louis Vuitton duffle over her right arm. She was staying it would seem.

So many emotions churned inside me and I just watched it all unfold. I didn't move to go find Creed. I didn't walk toward my house. I wasn't sure I could. This wasn't what I was expecting to see. He had said the ball was in my court and after a week of no communication he is back to his old girlfriends…or had he ever stopped them?

Creed walked out the back door this time and was headed toward his Jeep when his gaze landed on me standing there at the end of his driveway. I was sure I looked as lost as I felt. I didn't belong here. I hadn't been invited yet I watched him.

He didn't make a move toward me but I heard a female voice call out something and Creed looked back over his shoulder and replied. I was too far away to hear what was being said. I was thankful for that. One less thing to haunt my dreams. I needed to make my legs work and start home.

Dropping my gaze to the ground and away from his, I managed to start moving again. My legs felt heavy and everything my dad had said seemed pointless now. The last time I'd been broken over Creed Sullivan no one had been able to fix me but Griff. I didn't even have that now. I didn't deserve it.

"Sailor." Creed's voice stopped me from walking in the house just as I opened the door. I glanced over my shoulder to see him in my backyard. He'd stopped coming near me, but he was close enough that I could hear him easily enough. "I gave you time."

I laughed then. Loudly and slightly frantic. "A week. You gave me a week," I told him then shook my head in disbelief. Did he honestly think that was a good excuse? He had been in my house having sex with me less than two weeks ago and now he is having a sleep over with Ember. No. I was not okay with this.

"You went to Boston last night," he said with clear accusation in his tone.

Angry now, I turned completely around to face him. "Yeah, I did. How the hell do you know where I went?"

He shrugged. "Does that matter? It's a fact."

I glared at him and took a step in his direction. "My going to Boston to spend time with my father who I never see is reason enough for you to bring that woman back to your house? Right under my nose? I'm sorry, Creed, that I made you wait a week then spent time with my dad. Please forgive me!" I was yelling now and I didn't even care. It felt good. I needed to scream.

"I thought you were with Griff," he said.

"I know exactly what you thought, Creed. But no. I cheated on Griff with you. Sweet, kind, loving Griff who would move mountains for me. I chose you. Not my brightest moment," I said it before I could stop myself and I saw him wince. I wasn't one to say things to hurt others, but I wanted Creed to hurt. He'd hurt me and I wanted to hurt him.

Creed looked away from me and shoved his hands deep into the pockets of his leather coat. He said nothing and I didn't know what else to say. A large portion of me wanted to apologize for what I said but the other part was too selfish.

"Why don't you think about this, Sailor, if Griff is so fucking perfect then why wasn't he making time to see you? Call you? If what you had was so great, why did you have sex with me? I can't think of one damn thing the guy did for you that was selfless. Maybe if you'd open your eyes and," he stopped then and closed his mouth. Shaking his head, he turned and headed back toward his house.

"Say it!" I called out to him. Whatever it was and however hurtful it would be, I wanted him to say it. If just to make us even.

He paused and turned back to me. "I didn't sleep with Ember. I was never planning on it." He said nothing more then turned and started walking away again. No more words. No more anger. He was just gone.

twenty-eight

NOVEMBER 26, 2019

With no work this week, because the museum was closed for Thanksgiving week, I decided to decorate for Christmas and start buying some gifts. Today I had spent five hours buying more decorations than my house needed. I didn't care, the retail therapy was good for me. While walking the aisles of Christmas cheer and listening to the holiday music over the speakers, it had made me forget for a moment that I was once again a broken lonely woman.

I was on my second trip to the car to unload when Margie came walking up my drive.

"Looks like someone is about to deck the halls," she said cheerfully.

"I'm off work this week and thought I'd get started."

She beamed. "I need to do the same but the boys are coming home and Dan has his wife and kids, then Dale has a new boyfriend we can't wait to meet. Anyway, I was wondering if you had spoken to Creed lately."

I shook my head no.

She sighed and looked at his house with a small frown. "Well, Dan and his wife were set to lease his house starting in December, but he canceled on them and said he was moving into it a few weeks ago. We were happy he was going to be home and understood; however, he's not there much anymore and I was wondering if he decided to take that opportunity he had been given in England. Some architect school or something, I don't know. It was a big deal and just like with the house, he changed his mind. If he is going to leave the country, which Dale said it would be a chance of a lifetime for Creed in his career path, then I just wanted him to know Dan and Heather are still very interested in his house. Could you mention it if you see him?"

I had no words. Nothing she was saying made sense but then it did. If it made the sense I thought it did…if I understood what I was hearing…no. I had to be wrong. I managed a nod and a smile.

"Thanks so much. Happy Thanksgiving!" she said with a wave then headed back across the street.

I left the decorations in my car and walked to the backyard to stare at his house. He wasn't home. He hadn't been for several days.

Why had he decided to stay in Portsmouth when he could be doing something much bigger in England? What had changed a few weeks ago to make him abruptly come here and drop his other plans?

I was the only thing I knew of that had happened to him this past month. Wasn't I? Was I being self-absorbed to assume he was staying here for me? He'd barely been around me when he would have made these decisions. How could his change in plans be because of me? I didn't see how it was possible. Yet…

Reaching into the pocket of my coat, I pulled out my cellphone and found his number. My finger hovered over the call button, but I pressed message instead.

"When will you be home?"

I waited and when he didn't respond right away, I felt the heaviness that lived in my chest these days just get worse. He was probably off with Ember or Stormie celebrating the holiday week. I was being ridiculous. There was no way that he had changed his path to move in next door just to be near me. His feelings didn't run that deep. If they had, he wouldn't have walked away so easily. Griff had fought for me. He'd tried. Creed had done nothing. That was not a man who gave up an amazing opportunity and stayed in Portsmouth, NH.

I went back to the car and finished unloading it. The small thrill I'd gotten at the idea of making the house warm and full of holiday joy was gone. I had no desire to decorate anything, but I moved it all in the house and went inside to stare a fire.

I considered calling my mother and seeing if she was going to be in Nashville for Thanksgiving. The idea of going back there made me feel even more depressed but staying here all week by myself didn't sound like a great idea either. There was only so much decorating and Christmas shopping I could do.

Deciding I would just get up and drink my sorrows away, I was almost in the kitchen when there was a knock on the door. The second of hope that it was Creed came and went quickly. If it was Creed, then what was I going to say? Was there any point?

Slowly I made my way to the door and opened it.

Creed's hair was pulled back in a low ponytail that it was just long enough to make. His cheeks were red from the cold and he looked tired. "I'm home now," he replied.

I nodded and glanced back inside the house then at him. "Do you want to come inside?" I asked.

He didn't say anything at first and I was preparing myself for him to say no when he finally took a step in the door and I moved back out of his way. I closed the door behind him and he didn't walk in any farther. He stood there looking at me. Waiting on me. Which was fair since I had been the one to text him.

"Margie came by today looking for you," I said, not sure how to ask what I wanted to know.

He said nothing.

"Her son is still interested in your house," I continued and his eyes gave little away. "Creed, why did you decide to move into the house? Why didn't you go to England?"

His shoulders lifted and fell with a heavy sigh. Then he locked his gaze on mine. "Because of you."

All the words I wanted to say, all the questions I had, seemed to melt away as I stood there looking back at him. I managed a "Why?" because I didn't understand it. I didn't understand him.

"Why?" he repeated then he gave a small shake of his head. "You want to know why," he continued. "Fine. I'll tell you why, Sailor. I fell in love with a girl when I was ten years old. She was all I wanted in life. We got older and she was everything to me. She was so much to me that I could see nothing but her. I didn't notice when my twin sister was hurting. I didn't see the changes in her because all I could see was you. Then we found her. She was gone. I was seventeen and I blamed myself and I blamed you for making me love you so damn much. Seeing you reminded me of her and how I'd failed her. I believed that if I denied myself the one girl I knew I would always love that maybe I could forgive myself."

My eyes were burning and I blinked, not wanting the tears to fall. My hands were tightly fisted at my sides and breathing hurt so badly.

"Then you came back. I had my future all laid out and you walked into the room and nothing else mattered to me. Just like that it was all there roaring to the surface and the worst part was you weren't mine. You were his. I'd lost you. Leaving for England would have been the smart thing for me to do but you're right. I'm not selfless. I am fucking selfish. I canceled it all so I could be near you."

I felt a sob escape me and I covered my mouth to keep it quiet. This was not what I'd expected to hear from him when

I'd asked. This was rawer than anything we'd ever said to each other. All the darkness, the pain, the destruction was laid bare with the truth.

Creed ran a hand over his face. "I can honestly say that I didn't stay here to ruin your relationship. I didn't want to cause you any pain. I wanted to be near you. I needed to be near you. But I also can't tell you I didn't want you for myself. Because I did. I always have. I wish I could regret it, feel bad for it, but I can't. I love you, Sailor Copeland, and I fucking always will. I've tried not to. I've done everything in my power not to love you and I failed."

My face was wet with tears and I didn't wipe them away. He'd said everything I had needed him to say. He'd answered every question I had ever had about us. Yet to give me that truth, it had hurt him. I moved toward him, only knowing I wanted to comfort him.

He stiffened and I stopped. Lifting my eyes to his I studied his expression. He was no longer able to keep it closed off, not now that he'd said all he had. His secrets were no more.

"Why didn't you fight for me then? When I told you Griff came, you didn't even listen to me or talk to me."

"Sailor, you've told me you loved him. I wanted you to be sure it was me you loved more. I didn't want to force you to choose me when I was the one who shut you out six years ago. It was your choice. No matter how bad it would destroy me. I had to let you make it."

I closed the space between us then and wrapped my arms around his waist, pressing my face against his chest. His arms wrapped around me tightly and held me there. We didn't say anything for several minutes and I didn't think words needed to be said.

He had always been my choice, but until now, I hadn't realized I was his. My not knowing why or how he felt led me to not trust him.

"The night Griff came here, he said he'd seen you at the bar. A girl was in your lap." I had to get that out. It was the only other thing standing between me truly being able to trust Creed.

"And he came straight here and told you that?"

I nodded.

Creed shook his head with a scowl. "Son of a bitch," he muttered.

I liked Griff's mother and she wasn't a bitch, but I didn't think that was the point to his cursing. I kept my mouth closed and waited.

"Sailor, that was Rachel. She was flying out of Boston the next morning and was at the bar to hear me play before she left. She had sat in my lap because it kept the girls who were coming over away from me. I'd been asked to sign several body parts that night and Rachel fixed the problem."

Griff hadn't lied. He just hadn't known the truth. "I'm sorry I didn't ask you before."

"He's not perfect. He's a nice guy, but he's also self-absorbed and selfish."

I didn't feel the need to defend Griff. He wasn't a part of our equation anymore. Yes, he'd saved me when I needed saving but that was a chapter in my life that was now closed. He wasn't the guy I had loved anymore. I would always care for Griff. He'd been an important part of my life for four years. But that was over now.

"Stay with me?" I asked him.

"With you is the only place I have ever wanted to be," he replied.

twenty-nine

NOVEMBER 28, 2019

The kitchen was a mess and I had made it that way. Determined to bake something for Thanksgiving dinner at Creed's mother's house had caused me more stress than I expected. I had gone through all of Gran's Thanksgiving recipes and settled on pecan pie. I didn't know how difficult pecan pie could be or how hard it was to find pecans at the store. Apparently, there was a shortage.

Pulling out the pecan pie from the oven, I sighed in relief that this one had turned out good. I'd burned the last one because I had misread the directions and set the oven too hot.

"Smells good," Creed said, as he walked into the kitchen door from getting more firewood. He'd been going over to get firewood from his house more and more. We spent most of our time at Gran's house and I required more heat than he did.

"This one worked!" I exclaimed as I sat it down on a pot holder.

"Is it vegan?" he asked me.

I glanced back at him over my shoulder. His hair was wind-blown and the stubble on his jawline gave him a rugged sexy look. "Yes," I replied.

"Don't tell anyone," he said with an amused grin.

"Vegan pecan pie is just as good as regular," I told him, although I wasn't exactly sure that was true. I'd never had Gran's pecan pie. The holidays she'd come to visit us, she never had the chance to cook or bake. My mother had everything catered.

"You saying pecan will distract anyone from the taste if it's bad," he said then and sat the wood down in the holder by the stove.

"YOU are the one saying it wrong," I told him.

He raised his eyebrows when he turned to look back at me. "Oh really? You do realize New England is where Thanksgiving started."

I was almost positive they didn't have pecan pie on the first Thanksgiving. Creed walked over to me and pulled me against him. He smelled incredible and because of that I could overlook the fact he was cold. I shivered but snuggled closer to him.

"You do know the way y'all say it is kind of gross," I teased, scrunching my nose in distaste. "PEE-can? Seriously? I doubt our ancestors called them that."

He chuckled then and bent down to kiss the tip of my nose. "That's fine. Take your pick-AHN pie and make sure to call it that for my family's amusement."

"It's pee-KAHN" I corrected him.

He began trailing kisses from my temple down to my jawline and pecan pie didn't seem very important anymore. "I like the way you talk," he whispered near my ear. "I always have."

I shivered again but not from the cold. He was warm now and his hands were moving down my back to cover my bottom.

"Seems to be," he said, as he began tugging up my hoodie. "I like every fucking thing about you."

I lifted my arms up and he removed my top then he shrugged out of his jacket and pulled me back against him again. "I can't do much without thinking about you," he said, then his mouth covered mine and I went on my tiptoes, so I could reach him better.

His hands cupped my butt and picked me up then set me down on the kitchen counter. I was too close to hot pie but then he took off his shirt and I was distracted. His bare chest would distract anyone. I reached out and ran my hand down it, stopping just at the waist of his jeans. Lifting my eyes to his, I smiled wickedly at him then slid off the counter and went down to my knees.

I'd thought about doing this. Many daydreams in the shower I had done just this to him, but every time I got a chance, he always did something to make me forget my name.

"Sailor," he said my name with a husky groan, as I unzipped his jeans and tugged them down his hips along with his boxer briefs. Glancing up at him, I took his erection in my hand and pressed a small kiss to the tip.

He let out a low hard chuckle. "Jesus, woman."

Enjoying the power I suddenly had, I leaned forward and slid him into my mouth. One of his hands touched the back of my head as he made an appreciative sound in his throat. I began working my mouth and hand over him in the same rhythm as when we had sex. The noises he made were the best part of the experience. Creed made me crazy with things he did to my body and knowing I could do the same to him was thrilling.

"Sailor," he said my name on a plea. "I'm not going to make it much longer."

Understanding what he was telling me didn't slow me down or cause me to stop. I wanted to feel him break apart like this.

"Baby," he groaned and his hand fisted in my hair. His body began to tremble and I prepared myself for what was to come. Literally.

"Fuuuuuck," he shouted and I held onto him, making sure he received ever moment of pleasure. When he finally jerked as if he was suddenly very sensitive, I let him go and looked up at his face from my spot on the floor.

He was staring down at me with complete adoration and I grinned. I wiped the corner of my mouth with my fingers and stood up.

"Did I mention how much I love you?" he asked, and I burst out laughing as he pulled me against him. "No, I'm serious, I worship you," he said, and my laughter continued.

We stood there in the warmth of the kitchen with the aroma of pecan pie surrounding us for several moments. Creed didn't just make me happy; he made me complete. Most of my life I had wandered through it never feeling like I belonged anywhere. Until Creed.

"Thank you," I said, resting my head against his chest.

"Baby, I think I'm the one who is supposed to be thanking you," he replied.

Smiling, I pressed a kiss to his bare chest. "I'm serious."

"So am I," he said. "Completely serious. I've never been more serious."

I laughed softly then leaned back, so I could look up at his beautiful face. "Thank you for loving me. Life without you always felt like I was searching. When all along I just needed you."

He bent his head until his forehead touched mine.

"Loving you has always been my weakness," he replied.

Sighing, I hugged him tightly. "I need to go get a shower. We have to leave in an hour," I said, stepping back out of his arms reluctantly.

He smirked and glanced at the stairs. "I need a shower too."

I shook my head. "No. We will be late," I said, wishing we had time. Shower sex with Creed was my favorite.

"It's fine. I'll tell them we got hung up in the shower having hot soapy sex."

I slapped his chest. "No! You won't."

He shrugged. "We can tell them you had a problem with the pee-KAHN pie," he said then winked at me. "Come on, you know you want to."

Of course, I wanted to.

thirty

DECEMBER 14, 2019
BOSTON, MASSACHUSETTS

Being back in Boston was one thing, being back at Red's was another. Creed hadn't wanted to come do this gig tonight if I didn't come with him. Considering what had happened the last time he played with Kranx at Red's. It had been a month since I'd broken things off with Griff and it wasn't likely he'd even be at the bar tonight. Unless he had stopped studying all the time, which I very much doubted.

We had gotten in traffic on our drive here and had arrived just before the band went on stage. The large round booth in the corner was all mine. I sipped my martini and listened to the band glad I had come. I enjoyed watching Creed play and the last time I'd been here, I had tried my hardest not to watch him. Now I was free to soak it all in.

Red's was filled with colorful lights strung across the ceiling, in no particular order, and a Christmas tree had been added to the entrance. They even had an eggnog cocktail on their menu I wondered if anyone was ordering. Creed had ordered a large basket of fries and a grinder then left them for me. I hadn't known what a grinder was until the sub sandwich arrived with the fries. I took a fry just as Creed looked in my direction and winked. Smiling, I took a bite and enjoyed having his attention.

Although Red's didn't have a fireplace, like Clarks did, they were on the water or the marsh. Creed had corrected me when I called it the lake. I didn't know there was a difference. Glancing over my shoulder, I looked out at the lights from Red's twinkling on the water. Boats were anchored outside, but no one was on them. It was too cold for boating I would assume, but then this was New England and these people wore shorts when it was forty-five degrees out.

Relaxing, I leaned back with my cocktail and considered taking a bite of the sandwich when I glanced up to see Chet enter the bar. I'd hoped this wouldn't happen. I had almost convinced myself I was in the clear. Most college students were taking exams, so Chet and Griff should be studying. Creed had offered to call Chet and see if they were coming, but I'd felt bad asking him to do that. I would have to see Griff again, and if that was tonight, I would deal with it.

There was no Griff behind Chet though. I sighed in relief and decided I was taking a bite of the sandwich. If Chet was here and Griff wasn't with him then I was in the clear. This wasn't Griff's kind of place. He had never loved going to bars, but he'd go with me to listen to music when we were in Nashville.

Chet was talking to a small group of people and a pretty brunette was with him. I wondered if that was Shelly and the idea made me grin. Moving my eyes back to Creed on stage he was watching me. I wondered if he'd seen Chet enter too and had waited to see if Griff followed. I held up my drink to him in a toast and he smirked.

They would hopefully be getting a break soon. I missed him.

"Hey, Sailor," Chet said, and I had missed his walking over here toward me. He'd been at Thanksgiving, and after he made a joke about me switching boyfriends, we had all been comfortable.

"Hello, Chet," I replied. "Y'all want to sit here? The place is packed."

Chet motioned for the brunette to slide inside the booth before him. "Thanks, I was hoping you'd offer. If not, I was just going to be rude and sit. Sailor, this is Maegan, and Maegan, this is Sailor."

Maegan's eyes went wide and I was preparing myself for her to recognize me as Denver Copeland's daughter when she said, "So you're *the* Sailor?"

"Oh yeah, that's her," Chet replied grinning wickedly. "Griff was drinking too much this evening and went on a drunken rant about you. I wasn't sharing your shit or anything," he said to me.

I hated to think of Griff getting drunk. It wasn't like him. Although I didn't love Griff, I cared about him. He had been important to me for four years. Breaking up with him didn't change that.

"I'm surprised he was drinking with exams," I said.

"We are done. He's heading back to Nashville tomorrow for the holiday break. Instead of going out tonight, he decided to have his own party with Jim Bean," Chet said then reached for the fry basket. "Do you mind?" he asked, before taking a fry.

I shook my head. "Take all you want."

"Is the grinder not good?" he asked me, nodding toward the sub.

"It's okay."

"Which one is Creed?" Maegan asked.

Chet smirked at me then looked at his date. "The wicked hot one," he said.

Maegan didn't have a hard time figuring that out. "Oh," she replied, and I knew what she was thinking. Yes, Creed was beautiful and sexy but that hadn't been why I chose him over Griff. I couldn't exactly defend my choice though she wasn't voicing her thoughts.

"Well damn," Chet said, his attention on the door.

I followed his gaze. "Oh no," I whispered.

Griff had decided to come out after all. Even if Chet hadn't told me he was drunk, I'd have been able to tell. Especially when he looked our way and raised his hand to wave it back and forth in the air at us and shout. "HEY!"

Griff did not cause scenes. At least he didn't sober. The amount of times I had witnessed Griff even tipsy I could count on one hand. His dad was a recovering alcoholic and Griff drank in moderation.

"Didn't think he was going to leave," Chet said, looking unsure on what to do.

"Did he drive here?" Maegan asked sounding horrified.

"Fuck, I hope not," Chet said and stood up as Griff started making his way toward us.

Griff stumbled twice and bumped into people that he then stopped to apologize to and point at our table before continuing on. I had to do something, but I didn't know what to do. I moved to the edge of the booth, in case I needed to stand up and get Griff out of the bar.

"What a coincidence," he slurred loudly when he reached us.

"You're drunk, Griff. We need to take you back to the apartment," Chet said, standing up and putting a hand on his chest to keep him from falling into the table.

"I'm fine! Here to party. Ain't that why you're here, Sailor?"

I looked at Chet unsure if I should even speak. He rolled his eyes at Griff and tried to turn him around. "If I don't get you out of here, you are going to regret it in the morning," Chet told him. "Trust me."

Griff jerked away from Chet and almost fell on top of me. He caught himself on the back of the booth, but he was leaning over me and laughing as he steadied himself. "Hello Sailor," he said grinning. "Are you here to see your boyfriend play?" he asked then leaned down closer to me. "Guess you realized you had to come with him to keep him from fucking someone else."

I opened my mouth to tell him to shut up when he was jerked away. Creed had the back of Griff's shirt in his fist and the fury on Creed's face scared me.

"He's drunk!" I said, as I hurried to get out of the booth and stop this. "He doesn't mean anything he's saying, Creed."

"She's right. He's had a fifth of Jim Bean this afternoon," Chet said, sounding as worried as I was.

"There are some right and wrong answers here," Griff slurred, still grinning while Creed held him up. "I have indeed drunk a fifth of Jim, but I do know what I'm saying."

"Shut up, Griff!" Chet said, moving toward Creed. "Give him to me. I will take him to the apartment."

"The apartment!" Griff shouted. "I don't want to go to the apartment. Tell me Creed, did you start fucking my girlfriend at the apartment or did y'all wait until you were in Portsmouth?"

"I don't give a fuck if you're drunk. If you say one more word about Sailor, I will beat your face in," Creed warned in a low voice, loud enough for us to hear.

Griff cackled like an idiot. "You took my girl. What more can you do to me? Tell me, Sailor, is the sex that good?"

Creed threw him then and Griff went face forward into the wall.

I screamed, and Chet cursed loudly.

"Creed! Stop!" I begged, as Griff got his bearings and turned around to look at Creed. He wasn't smiling anymore.

"What happens when you get bored with her? When the sex gets old and you want something new?" Griff taunted him and I reached out to grab Griff before he got any closer to Creed.

I wasn't fast enough. Creed's fist connected with Griff's face and he went down again.

"CREED!" I screamed in horror, just as the bouncer arrived to take Creed's arms and restrain him. I fell to my knees and checked to make sure Griff was breathing because he was unconscious.

"Do I need to call an ambulance?" a waitress asked, standing over us.

I shook my head. "I don't know," I told her honestly.

Chet was beside me then and I was thankful for his medical knowledge. My heart was pounding from fear.

"His pulse is steady," Chet said and glanced at me.

"That's good, right?" I asked, twisting my hands in my lap nervously.

He nodded. "Yeah. He's probably going to have a concussion from the way he hit his head when he fell. As long as I watch him tonight and check his vitals regularly, I think he's okay to go home."

"I'm going with you," I said, needing to help somehow.

Chet frowned and glanced back at the door where the bouncer had taken Creed. "I don't know if Creed will be okay with that."

"I don't care what Creed is okay with. You can't stay up all night and watch him. We can take turns."

Chet sighed then nodded his head. "You're right. I've drank too much to stay awake all night."

"I can help too," Maegan offered, and I remembered she was here. Glancing at the rest of the bar, I realized people were all standing around watching us.

Jazz's eyes met mine and she was glaring at me. I'd messed up their night. They were out a guitar player. I didn't have time to worry about the band or anyone else for that matter. I had to help get Griff out of here and deal with Creed. What in the world had he been thinking? It was obvious Griff was drunk. Besides that, I'd told him several times.

Griff grunted then and I swung my gaze back down to him.

"He's coming around. That's good," Chet said and leaned forward to put his hand under Griff's back. "Come on, you need to sit up slow," he told him.

"Where's the fucker at?" he slurred worse than he had been before.

"He's gone. Now if you can keep your mouth shut we might get you home before he kills you," Chet told him.

Griff squinted at me. "What are you doing?"

"Helping," I replied.

"I don't want your help," he said.

"She's helping me," Chet told him. "Just shut the hell up and focus on standing."

"I'll go get the car and bring it around to the front," Maegan said.

"Thanks," Chet told her but kept his eyes on Griff, who was struggling to get to his feet.

I stood up and grabbed my coat and purse from the booth then followed them as Chet held Griff steady with his arm around his back as they went to the exit.

A waitress hurried toward us. "If one of you can sign this on his behalf. It's stating he refused medical attention," she explained. Chet nodded at me and I took the paper, signed it and handed it back to her.

"I'm a fucking doctor. I don't need medical attention," Griff said.

"You're right. You need mental attention," Chet said sourly as we walked into the cold night air.

My eyes found Creed. He was leaning against his Jeep with his arms crossed over his chest looking furious. He wasn't going to like my going to help but I had to. Chet couldn't do this alone and I felt responsible for the entire thing.

Chet stopped beside Creed and covered Griff's mouth with his free hand to keep him from saying something stupid. "You're an ass," Chet told Creed as Maegan pulled the car up beside us.

"I'm going with them," I told Creed.

"What?" he asked, the anger changing to hurt quickly.

"Chet needs my help. I can't. I don't." I stopped and shook my head, trying to find the words. "I can't believe you did this, Creed. I'm not okay with it."

"Did you not hear what he was saying?" Creed asked me.

"He is drunk. Drunk!" I yelled the last part. "I need to go help them and I need some space right now. Tomorrow. We will talk about this tomorrow," I said then turned and climbed into the front seat beside Maegan who was driving. I didn't look back at Creed as we drove away, but my stomach felt sick leaving him like that. He had been stupid tonight and I would forgive him. For now, I needed to be mad for a little bit. He would have to wait until I was calm enough to talk to him. Tomorrow, when Griff was fine, then I would be ready to talk this over with Creed. He couldn't go smashing a guy's face in because he said something about me or to me that wasn't nice. I was not a fan of violence. I understood that he was upset with the things Griff had said but Griff was drunk. He was also still hurting. A hurt that I had caused him. I felt the guilt of that weighing on me. Maybe it wasn't Creed I was mad at…maybe it was me.

thirty-one

DECEMBER 15, 2019
BOSTON, MASSACHUSETTS

"Sailor," a voice broke into my dreams and I felt my shoulder being shaken. I struggled to open my eyes. It had been a long night, and I'd slept very little. Even when it was my turn to sleep, I had been unable to because I was worried about Creed. Last night's events came back to me and my chest felt heavy again.

Opening my eyes, I saw Chet, looking as bad as I felt, standing over me. I had fallen asleep in the chair and it had been my turn to stay awake and watch Griff. Sitting up, I looked around. "Oh no, I'm sorry!" I hadn't meant to fall asleep.

"Sailor," he said again in a serious tone. I looked at him closer then and saw dark circles under his eyes.

"Is he okay?" I asked, then jumped out of my chair to head to Griff's bedroom. The door was closed. I had left it open.

"Sailor," Chet said again. "Griff is fine."

I sagged in relief and turned back to him with a tired smile. "Oh. Whew. I didn't mean to fall asleep on my watch. What time is it?" I asked him, realizing it had to be late since the sun was bright outside.

"I need you to sit down," Chet said then and a tiny bubble of fear began to grow inside my chest.

"Why? What's wrong? You said he was okay," I reminded him, not understanding why Chet looked so damn upset.

"Please, sit," he said the words too gently then.

I did as he requested because I needed an answer. My panic was rising by the second.

"The police just left," he said.

"Why?" I asked slowly. Had they arrested Creed? Griff hadn't pressed any charges.

Chet ran a hand over his face and I saw unshed tears in his eyes.

"Chet, tell me what is wrong, now," I demanded.

He took a deep breath and walked over to me then bent down in front of me and took both my hands. "They found Creed's Jeep," he began, but as understanding started dawning on me, I shook my head and stood up pushing him back.

"No, they didn't," I said and walked over to the fireplace, needing some space to breathe. It felt small in here suddenly. Not large enough for two people. The walls felt as if they were closing in on me.

"It was in the marsh, Sailor. Deep."

"NOOOO!!!" I screamed then and bent over, not wanting him to finish. I could not listen to this. I refused to. It was a nightmare and I needed to wake up. I was exhausted and when I didn't get enough sleep, I had terrible dreams.

A hand touched my shoulder and I jerked away from it. "They can't find the body," he said then and I stood up gasping for air.

"He's okay then. He got out," I said, wanting to cry from relief. Why hadn't he told me that first?

"They think he tried…but he was very drunk. The last person to see him was Dalm and he said he thought Creed was staying the night at their place. They didn't know he had left until the cops arrived there looking for him three hours ago."

"He got out," I repeated, hating Chet for saying otherwise. Creed was not in that Jeep. He was alive.

"They've checked all the hospitals and hotels nearby, they've even called his mother and she's checked his house. There would have been no way for him to get that far anyway. There weren't even hotels near where he drove into the water and it was after two this morning when it happened."

I refused to stand here and listen to this. "They didn't find a body. He will show up today. He's alive." I moved past Chet to get my coat and my purse. I was leaving. I'd go find him myself.

"Sailor, where are you going?" he asked.

"I'm going to find Creed," I stated the obvious.

"The marsh is deep where he went in but his Jeep didn't sink all the way because the back wheels were stuck in the mud. He was drunk, and if he managed to get out, he sank. A part of his shirt was torn and stuck to the doorframe."

I held up my hands. "STOP TALKING!" I yelled. I needed him to stop telling me all the ways Creed couldn't have survived.

The door to Griff's room opened. "What's going on?" he asked in a gruff whisper then winced from the sound.

"Nothing. I am leaving," I said and spun around to open the door and get out of this apartment.

"Sailor, you don't have a car, and even if you did, you are in no state to drive," Chet said walking toward me.

"I can call an Uber," I told him, ready to run if I had to in order to get out of this apartment.

"The cops," he started to say.

"KNOW NOTHING. Creed is not…he is not…" I couldn't' finish that sentence. My knees went weak then and I grabbed the door knob to hold myself up.

Chet was there then, helping me stand and moving me back toward the sofa. A sob tore from my chest and I crumbled onto the worn leather, my body wracking uncontrollably with sobs.

I heard Chet and Griff talking, but I couldn't focus on their words.

I felt the sofa sink as someone sat down beside me.

"What can I do?" Griff asked.

"Nothing. I just need Creed to wake up and let us know where he is," I said, not looking at him. I stayed in a fetal position and tried to process what I knew. There was no body. I held onto that as tightly as I could. It was all that kept me from falling apart. Creed wouldn't leave me.

"What can we do?" Griff then asked Chet.

"We wait. If he's alive, we will know soon enough. If there is a way," he paused then. "If he's out there, he'll show up."

I hated Chet for saying "if." I hated myself for coming here last night. I hated Griff for showing up drunk and causing this all to happen. I hated the police for believing Creed couldn't have gotten out of the Jeep.

Why hadn't he stayed at Dalm's? I told him that we would talk tomorrow. I told him I just needed some space. Why didn't he just wait?

The day went on, and Creed never showed up. The Coast Guard began dragging the marsh and my world became a dark place I no longer recognized. I had lost Creed when I was seventeen and a miracle brought him back to me. Life was cruel and cold. It only gave me complete joy long enough for me to know what it felt like, before snatching it away from me.

How did one find joy again after losing their soulmate? It had been easier when I lost him the first time because I knew he still lived. His light was still shinning and I could accept a life without him if he was alive. However, how did I go on with him gone from this world?

The pain that came with the setting of the sun, knowing he wasn't coming back, was beyond any hurt that I had ever known. It was a despair so deep I didn't want to find the light. I would sink into it until I was numb. It was the only way I knew I could survive.

thirty-two

DECEMBER 16, 2019
BOSTON, MASSACHUSETTS

Twenty-Four hours. It had been twenty-four hours since I'd been woken up to hear Chet tell me Creed had drowned. For those twenty-four hours, I had stayed strong. I had believed he would show up. That he would explain it all.

Now, I stood at the spot where they pulled his Jeep from the water as the icy wind dried my tears. He hadn't called. His phone was found in the Jeep but still no word from him. He hadn't checked into a hotel and his credit cards hadn't been used. Every ounce of hope I had held onto so tightly seemed to wash away with the water in front of me.

My knees buckled and I welcomed the ground beneath me. How was I supposed to go on tomorrow and the next day? My heart had been shattered before, but it had never been taken from me. This was a level of pain I didn't know existed. The hell that Albert had mentioned all made sense to me now.

"Sailor," Chet's voice called out to me, but I refused to look back at him. Every time he looked at me, I saw the truth. He had accepted Creed was gone. He had from the very beginning. I hated to see that in his eyes. He felt sorry for me. I could see that too.

"Sailor, you need to get inside and warm up. You are going to freeze out here," he said as his boots stopped in front of me. I stared at those boots so different from Creed's black ones. Creed wore black combat boots where Chet's were a soft brown suede that reminded me of a med student or a minister.

"Don't make me throw you over my shoulder. I can't let you freeze to death. Please come with me," Chet pleaded.

I lifted my head to look up at him. He was wearing a wool coat with a scarf wrapped around his neck. I wasn't wearing anything more than the gray sweatshirt he had given me earlier today. The biting cold hurt and I embraced the pain. I welcomed it. I wanted to hurt physically because the pain inside my body was more than I could bare.

"He's not coming back," I said the words for the first time aloud.

The corners of Chet's mouth turned down and he bent his knees until he was eye level with me. "I'm so sorry, Sailor." His words were sincere, filled with a pain of his own.

"Me too," I whispered then turned to look out at the water. I was sorry for so many things. The list of the things I was sorry for was so long I didn't want to think about them all.

"Come with me," he urged, holding out his hand. "We need to get you warm. Your lips are blue."

I didn't care about my lips. I didn't care about warmth. Nothing mattered anymore. It never would again. The future I had planned was gone. I was to live a life with an empty void in my chest where my heart once was.

Chet took my hand and pulled me up then began walking me toward his car. He didn't say anything more and I was thankful for that. I didn't want to hear it. I just wanted to figure out a way to survive in this agony that was now my life.

When I was safely inside the car, I felt feeling slowly come back to my hands and feet as we drove away. Chet reached into the backseat and pulled a blanket toward me. "Here, you need this," he said.

I took it and held it over me. The pain of the cold thawing left the horrible ache inside roaring all on its own. Living a life without Creed…I didn't want to think about it.

"Griff is worried about you. He wanted to come get you, but I told him it was best if I did. Maybe you could talk to him about this. He will listen. You need to talk and let some of this pain free."

I turned to look at Chet. He glanced at me then back to the road. He was a nice guy. I was glad Griff had him in his life. He, however, did not understand what I was experiencing. He meant well.

"Talking won't give me back my heart, Chet."

He looked pained as he turned back to me. He wanted to help and as kind as that was, there was nothing he nor anyone else could do. Creed was gone.

thirty-three

JULY 28, 2014
PORTSMOUTH, NH

Creed ended the kiss, but he left his forehead resting on mine as we both worked on catching our breath. Kissing Creed was one of my favorite things. Lately something else had taken the number one spot and if my Gran found out about it, I was sure I wouldn't get to see Creed again. Gran loved the Sullivans, but she wasn't going to be okay with her granddaughter having sex at seventeen.

"I want to take you to the barn," he whispered. Which was the closest spot for us to be alone.

I smiled and shivered from excitement. Hearing him want to be with me always made me feel giddy. "We haven't seen Cora all day," I reminded him. "I need to spend time with her too. We have barely seen each other this week."

Creed ran a finger down my cheek. "I don't want to share you," he admitted.

I sighed from the pleasure of his touch. "She's your sister."

He chuckled. "So, we've never shared well."

Knowing if we kept this up we wouldn't stop, I pushed back away from him. "I need to go inside your house and I don't want to be flushed when your momma sees me."

He smirked then. "My mom isn't here and I like it when you're flushed."

I opened the car door then and got out before I did something stupid like kiss him again. I had promised Cora we would go get manicures today. I wasn't about to cancel on her because I wanted to go have sex with her brother. That was just rude. I was a better friend than that.

Creed was out of the car and beside me before I got to the driveway. "Fine. Let's go visit my sister," he said with no enthusiasm.

"Not you. Just me," I reminded him. "It's a girl day. We are getting manicures"

"Our summer is running out. I don't want to give you up all day." His words made me sad. He was right and I hated the reminder. I also hated Nashville and being away from him. I'd begged Mom and Gran to let me finish my last year of high school in Portsmouth. Gran had agreed easy enough, but my mother was being more difficult.

There was always a good chance she'd give in though. "I may not have to leave this summer," I reminded him.

His hand grabbed mine. "God, I hope not. Having you all year would be fucking incredible. I'm just scared to get my hopes up."

When we reached the house, he opened the door for me then pressed a quick kiss to my lips. "Go do girl things with Cora. When you're done, you can find me in the game room."

I nodded then flashed one more smile his way, before heading to the stairs that led to Cora's bedroom.

"Hey, Sailor Moon," he called out and I looked back at him. "I love you."

His words sent a warm jolt of joy through me. He said it often now, but it never lost its power.

"I love you most," I replied, then hurried up the stairs before he could argue that.

High on love, I swung open Cora's bedroom door and announced "I'm here!" but realized she wasn't. Her Jetta was outside in the driveway, so she wasn't gone. I started to turn and go look for her in the rest of the house when I noticed a pill bottle on the floor and went over to pick it up.

My eyes went from the bottle to the other bottle beside her bed that was sitting on top of a letter. The writing was Cora's and I didn't want to invade her privacy, but I felt like it was a letter meant to be seen. I reached for it, and as I read the words, my stomach knotted up in fear.

I then saw the other bottle laying on her bed just under the pillow. Grabbing it and the one on the floor, I took the letter and ran from the room to find Creed. He was in the game room when I came barreling through the door.

"Sailor?" he asked, standing up from the sofa when he saw the look of horror I knew was clearly on my face.

"Cora," I said, handing him the letter as the pill bottles fell at our feet. "Oh god," I said as my hands shook uncontrollably.

Creed read the letter then looked at me. "Where is she?" he asked me. I saw the same fear spiraling out of control inside me reflected in his eyes.

"She's not in her room," I said then I knew. I knew where she had gone. It was where we always had gone as kids. She loved to go there to be alone and to tell me her wild adventures with boys. It was somewhere no one would look for us when we were younger.

Now, it was also where Creed and I went to have sex. "The barn," I blurted out. "She would go there." I was sure of it.

Creed broke into a run and I was right behind him. He swung open the door of the house, and we both raced outside, not bothering to go to the car but heading across the street and through the neighbor's yard. It was faster than driving. Horrible scenarios played out in my head and I refused to accept them. We would find her alive and stop her before she took the pills. The only problem with that hope was the bottles had already been emptied.

The faded red barn came into view on the abandoned property that remained in a trust belonging to some family in New York. In all the years of coming here, I'd never seen any of them here. The closer we got to the barn, the harder my heart slammed against my chest. She had to be alive.

"CORA!" Creed called out before we reached the two large doors that were firmly closed. "CORA!" There was a wild panic to his voice as he yelled out her name again.

Before he opened the doors, I knew. It was as if she was there with me, preparing me. The hope I'd had running here was gone. Snatched from me. I wanted to scream at the reality that was sinking in.

Creed jerked the door open and was inside several seconds before I reached the barn. I pushed myself harder. Faster. He didn't need to find her alone. I was inside seconds after him and I stopped before colliding with his body. He was standing just inside and three feet in front of him was Cora. Lifeless on the ground.

I moved around him and went to my knees beside her. "Cora." My voice cracked as I said her name loudly, as if I could wake her. I fumbled for a pulse and then placed my hand on her chest to find she wasn't breathing. I'd never taken CPR, but all I'd ever seen or read came back to me and I started trying to bring her back.

Tears streamed down my face and I wiped at them frustrated that it was hindering my vision. I began begging her to open her eyes and breathe. My voice was getting louder and my tears so heavy I couldn't see her clearly. I don't know how long I worked on her when I felt a hand on my shoulder. Looking back, thinking it was going to be Creed, I wiped at my face with my bare arm and realized it was Gran instead.

"Help her, Gran!" I begged and let out another sob. Gran pulled me into her arms and held me as I began to weep. Cora's skin had been so cold. Although I had known nothing I was doing would bring her back I had held onto every ounce of hope I could find. Facing the truth now was a horror I didn't want to accept.

I heard other voices and sirens and lifted my head to see who was here. Creed was standing in the doorway, staring at his sister, his face void of emotion. I wanted to go to him and comfort him. Pulling free of Gran, I stood up and his eyes shifted to me.

"Creed," I said his name on a sob and he stared at me for one brief moment then turned and walked out of the barn. Away from the scene in front of me. When the paramedics and her parents came rushing inside the barn, Creed didn't come back. He never came back.

epilogue

DECEMBER 17, 2019
BOSTON, MASSACHUSETTS

The water lapped against the shore as the northern wind blew. Forty-three hours had passed and the cold reality of my life was mocking me. I stared out at the water, hating it just as I hated everything else in this life. Finding beauty in this world had once been a passion of mine, but all I could see was the horror that laid beneath the surface. It showed no compassion as it continued to live on. Cars still drove down the street behind me, people still went to work, they sang Christmas carols, and went to parties.

Nothing stopped just because my world had been destroyed. Nothing cared that every day people lost someone they loved and nothing was ever the same. It was unfair to watch it happen and be the one lost in the middle of it all. I wanted to scream at them all to stop!

I wasn't the first person to experience this kind of suffering. I wouldn't be the last. Not every chapter ended happy in life and I wished my book was just over. I didn't care about the chapters to come. The only chapters I cared about were done. A memory now was all I had.

"It's not fair!" I screamed out over the water that had taken Creed from me. "Why didn't you stay safe? Why did you get in that stupid Jeep and drive drunk?" I called out. "You ruined my life. How do I go on without you? You were my anchor in this world." Tears streamed down my face as I let the angry words explode from me. "I told you that I just needed one night. That tomorrow we would talk. Tomorrow wasn't asking a lot. I love you, Creed Sullivan! Why couldn't you have just waited?"

Wrapping my arms around my waist, I bent forward and wept. I thought I heard footsteps behind me. If Chet had come to get me again, or Griff, I was going to scream. I didn't want to see them. I didn't want to see the sadness in their eyes and the worry when they looked at me.

"About tomorrow…," a deep achingly familiar voice said.

I lifted my head and looked out at the angry water, before turning around slowly. I was afraid of what I'd see. Was I dreaming again or hallucinating?

Covering my mouth, I let out a wail as Creed stood there in the same clothes he'd had on the night he drove into the water. His hair was a tangled mess and he looked exhausted.

"I'm here, Sailor," he said, moving toward me slowly. "It's a long story, but I can explain. I'm just sorry I couldn't get a message to you sooner. I'll never forgive myself for the pain you've been through."

I choked on a sob. "Is…is this a dream?" I asked. "Please don't be a dream. I can't take it if it is," I pleaded, reaching for him and finding a solid flesh and bone man. "You're real," I said with disbelief, looking up at him through my swollen eyes.

He pulled me into his arms and held me tightly. "God, Sailor, I am so sorry. I swear if I had known what the hell I was doing…I promise, I'll never drink again," he said, kissing the top of my head then keeping his mouth pressed there.

"How are you alive?" I asked, needing this to make sense. Needing this to be real and not a dream. I clung to his shirt and then looked down to see the part of it that had been torn. I reached for it and squeezed it in my hand.

"I did drive my Jeep into the water because I was too fucking drunk to see the road. I was coming to you. I couldn't go another minute, much less until the next day, to apologize and make sure you didn't hate me. But I didn't drown. It wasn't even sinking when I got out. When I used the car door to boost myself out of the water and onto land, it pushed the Jeep down and it began to sink. I stood there and watched it in my drunken stupor then started walking out to the dock because I saw a commercial fishing boat and thought I'd see if someone could let me use their phone since mine sank with the Jeep."

He sighed then and kissed my head again. I leaned back to look up at him, realizing this had to be real. I wasn't this creative and no dream could make this up. I'd thought of a lot of scenarios, but nothing he was telling me was one of those scenarios. Reaching up, I touched his face and inhaled deeply. He stunk like fish, but I didn't care.

"No one was awake on the boat and I went searching for someone to help me. I made it to the bottom of the boat where they kept their gear and coolers with their catch. Then the whiskey got to me and I guess I laid down and passed out. When I came to, the boat was moving. I made my way up to the deck and found Burt. He was the Captain and we had been on the water for ten hours, but before that, I'd been on the boat passed out for four hours. My guess is the rocking of the boat kept me asleep. Burt didn't have a working means of communication and there was no cell phone signal. We tried several times to get through and once we managed to contact the Coast Guard, but the signal was so bad they didn't understand what Burt was telling them.

"I had to wait until they did their drag and headed back. They were sympathetic, but I was also a drunk man who had stowed away on their boat. They weren't going to lose out on a paycheck to get me back to land. I even tried paying them off, but they said it was a good lesson for me to learn."

"They finished up in less time than normal, but we still had a fourteen-hour ride back. They just dropped me off three hours ago. Burt was finally able to get a working signal to the Coast Guard, about thirty miles out, and they got in contact with Chet. He's been trying to call you the past three hours but you didn't answer. I was going to have him come pick me up, but he said there was a good chance I'd find you here."

I stared up at him. "You're alive," was all I could say.

He smiled at me. "I just got you back, Sailor Moon. I'm not about to check out on life now."

A laugh bubbled up, and I let it free. It was a sound I never expected to make and the feeling of pure joy inside me was one I thought was gone. "Don't ever die on me again," I said with passion. "Next time I get to die."

He laughed then and kissed my lips hard. "You'll have to take me with you," he said against my mouth.

I decided we could be like *The Notebook* and go at the same time. I was good with that. We could grow old together and have a life full of ups and downs but always together. Even in the end.

"I don't think I hate life and this world after all," I told him.

"Good," he replied, smiling at me unsure what I meant.

"When I thought it had taken you from me, I hated it," I explained.

He nodded. "Yeah, I was hating it too knowing you didn't know where I was and with my Jeep being in the water, you could be assuming the worst."

I dug my fingers into his dirty hair and held him close to me. "I love you, Creed Sullivan. Even when I'm angry and even when you do something stupid. I love you, always."

He ran his hand over my hair. "Good. Because I'm sure I'll be stupid again. I'm a man. It happens." Then he pulled back so he could look at me. "You're my yesterday, today and tomorrow. You always have been and always will be."

MAY 19, 2012
PORTSMOUTH, NEW HAMPSHIRE

"What you doing, brother?" Cora asked in a sing-song voice that always meant she was about to be annoying.

"I'm sitting on the porch," I said, waving my hand out at the obvious.

"Sitting out here for a reason in particular?" she asked sweetly and plopped down beside me.

"No," I lied. I didn't want to talk about Sailor with my sister. She liked to embarrass me and I didn't need to give her any ammunition to do so.

"Huh, well I guess you don't care that Sailor arrives today. A week early." She said it as if I didn't know it. I had been texting with Sailor most of the day. I knew she was almost here.

"I didn't say that," I told her, hoping she wouldn't tell Sailor that.

"So, you aren't sitting on the porch waiting for Sailor to arrive?" she asked, as she leaned forward resting her elbows on her knees. "Because that's what I am doing."

Cora loved Sailor and I knew she missed her, but I had wanted to see her before Cora was there to interrupt. The other three seasons were so damn slow during the year. It felt like an eternity between the day at the end of August to the third week in May when Sailor came back. This year, I'd finally gotten a Facebook account, so I could be her friend and see her pictures. Problem was she never posted pictures. However, she had been at several events with her dad and those had made it on the news. I had cut three different pictures they'd published in the *Country Music Magazine* and kept them hidden in my room.

"You know I'm out here waiting on her. Stop being a brat."

Cora giggled then. "Are you *in love*, brother?" she teased.

Telling my sister that I loved Sailor was a bad idea. She couldn't keep her mouth shut but then I couldn't exactly lie either. I didn't want to lie about that. What I felt for Sailor was more real than anything I'd ever known. Problem was Sailor lived over a thousand miles away and she was gorgeous and lived a famous lifestyle I knew nothing about. Guys talked about her being hot online and in school. It was annoying to listen to. They didn't know her.

"You are in love," Cora said and sighed dramatically then leaned into me. "Ah, young love," she said then laughed.

I didn't look at her. Maybe if I ignored her, she would go away. It was unlikely but a guy could hope. Getting rid of Cora was like trying to make a puppy stop chewing things. She didn't give up.

"Just shut up about that," I said, glaring at her.

She gave me a mock frown while her eyes still twinkled. I looked past her and at Bee's house to see if they were there yet. Cora leaned over to block my vision and I scowled some more. "Could you go annoy the hell out of someone else?" I asked, shoving her out of the way, so I could see.

"I could, but this is more fun," she replied.

I didn't reply.

"She likes you," Cora whispered as if someone could hear her.

I jerked my gaze off Bee's house to look at my sister. "Who?" I asked, needing her to be specific.

"Bee," she replied then rolled her eyes. "Sailor, you idiot."

"How do you know?" I asked her, hope soaring in my chest.

"She asks about you, who you're dating, that kind of thing," Cora said.

"I text with her all the time. She never asks me those things," I said, not sure I believed my sister.

"Yes, you stupid boy because she can't ask you those things or you'll know she likes you."

I frowned. That made no sense. "Why doesn't she want me to know she likes me?" I asked.

Cora sighed and leaned back on her hands. "That's the way girls are. You have to make the first move, but I'd do it quick because Derek Young was telling some guys at the last baseball game that as soon as Sailor got back into town, he was asking her out."

Fuck no he was not. Derek Young didn't even know Sailor. I didn't care if he was older and had a sports car. He wasn't asking her out, and even if he did, she wouldn't go. She liked me. Cora said so.

"He's an ass," I said.

"He's older and sexy," Cora replied.

Shooting her another glare, I stood up ready to get away from my sister. Bee's Volvo pulled into the driveway then and I didn't move. She was here. The summer was beginning and this year it would be different. This year I was going to make Sailor fall in love with me.

"Showtime lover boy," Cora said then shoved me toward Bee's house. "Go on and give her a big welcome. I'll give you some time before I come see her. Make it count."

I glanced back at my sister then walked down the steps to the sidewalk.

Sailor opened the car door and stepped out. Her dark brown curls were wild and danced around her like a halo. She was the most beautiful girl I'd ever seen and she always had been. She lifted a hand and waved at me as our eyes met. One day that girl was going to be mine, and I would never let her go.

You can connect with Abbi online in several different ways. She uses social media to procrastinate.

Facebook: AbbiGlinesAuthor
Twitter: abbiglines
Instagram: abbiglines
Snapchat: abbiglines

about Abbi

Abbi Glines is a #1 New York Times, USA Today, Wall Street Journal, and International bestselling author of the Rosemary Beach, Sea Breeze, Vincent Boys, Boys South of the Mason Dixon, and The Field Party Series. She is also author to the Sweet Trilogy and the Black Souls Trilogy. She believes in ghosts and has a habit of asking people if their house is haunted before she goes in it. Her house was built in 1820 and she's yet to find a ghost in it but she's still looking. She drinks afternoon tea because she wants to be British but alas she was born in Alabama although she now lives in New England (which makes her feel a little closer to the British). When asked how many books she has written she has to stop and count on her fingers. When she's not locked away writing, she is entertaining her preschooler, she is reading (if the preschooler will leave her alone long enough), shopping online (major Amazon Prime addiction), running because she eats too many tacos, and planning her next Disney World vacation.

Made in the USA
Monee, IL
15 December 2021